ACQUISITION

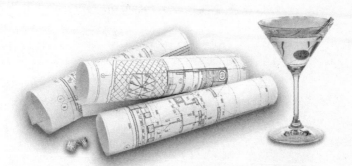

ACQUISITION

Cover Art by Okay Creations
Edited by Lisa A. Hollett
Proofread by Julie Deaton & Fiona Wilson
Interior Design by Chelle Bliss

www.chellebliss.com

ISBN-13: 978-1635761061
ISBN-10: 1635761069

First Edition

Dedication

Daddy, I'll forever be your little girl. Although you may not be by my side, you'll be forever in my heart.
— Chelle

"The supreme art of war is to subdue the enemy without fighting."

— Sun Tzu

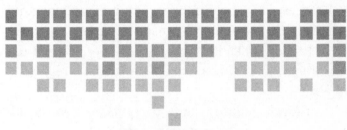

Prologue

Not many people can say that they're living their dream. I started on this path when I was only knee-high, but I never let anything stop me from achieving everything my father had planned for me.

When I was a little girl, my father and I would lie in the field behind our house for hours and stare at the night sky. He'd hold me close and point to the stars, twinkling like diamonds against black silk above us.

He dreamed of touching the heavens and visiting the vast reaches of space. He spent years studying to be an astronaut and almost achieved his goal. Tragically, within weeks of finishing training, a horrific car accident killed my mother and left him in a back brace for a year.

His career ended before it even began, and he changed his focus to me. He didn't force me onto the path I'm on now. No, my father taught me that I could achieve anything and believed I would touch the very reaches he'd always dreamed he would but never did.

"Lauren, your future is there," he'd say with wonder and excitement.

I'd look up, staring at the stars twinkling above us, and wonder what else was out there. Childhood curiosity and the love of my father drove me toward my destiny... toward today. Not into space, but to the inside of the boardroom, where I could make the dream a reality for others.

Although I didn't have the guts to become an astronaut, I knew from a young age that I wanted to make it possible for others to go where no man had gone before. My father believed in me and said I could do anything if I worked hard enough. I studied science and business at Boston University, graduating with a bachelor of science in aerospace and an MBA by the age of twenty-four.

It didn't matter that I was a woman in a male-dominated industry, the only limitations I had were those that others had placed on me, underestimating my drive and determination to reach the top.

Five years ago, I became the CEO of Interstellar Corp—one of the world's cutting-edge producers of aerospace technology. They are the second-largest company in the field, behind only Cozza International, the oldest company in the field. I never thought that within ten years of stepping through the door, I'd be head of the multibillion-dollar corporation.

I'd achieved a small piece of my father's dream before the age of thirty, but my father never got to see me take the helm. Three years before I was appointed the head of Interstellar, he died of a stroke

Although he wasn't standing by my side, I thought about him watching me from above, finally going to all the places he'd always dreamed of seeing.

It happened.

I'd made it.

Lauren Bradley, CEO of Interstellar Corporation.

But being a businesswoman and running a company had some major hurdles that I never expected.

But like with anything else in life, I didn't let it stop me.

I couldn't.

I always knew the business world would be cutthroat, but I never expected the betrayal to be from those closest to me.

I braced myself for it. There's always competition—both from inside the company and from other businesses in the same field.

Years before I became CEO, I made a mistake.

One that can be especially devastating to the career of a female executive.

Not a what, but a who.

Trent Moore.

We'd worked long hours together on the development of a new engine technology, and the lust became undeniable. It was my first big assignment for the company and the launching pad that catapulted me to the top. Between Trent's rugged good looks and MENSA-level genius, I couldn't help but be attracted to him.

He flirted.

I blushed.

He smiled.

I swooned.

After months of going back and forth, I gave in to him.

Relationships were a complication I couldn't afford, especially not in the beginning of my career. My mind knew it, but my body led me down the path of a sinful office romance that ended as spectacularly as a test rocket exploding before reaching the stratosphere.

Eventually, I came to my senses, feeling boxed in after he became possessive, which had me backpedaling and looking for a way out. After I was able to break off our relationship, I asked if we could be friends, but Trent refused to believe that we were over. He did everything in his power to get me back, and every time I told him no, he took it to mean yes.

I refused his every advance, but he bided his time and thought I'd come to my senses—but I never did.

The one thing I know about myself is that once my mind is made up, I never go back.

Trent was a hard lesson to learn—never mix business with pleasure. Interoffice romances spell disaster and should be avoided at all costs. I couldn't just walk away from him entirely. We worked together. And that there is the rub.

When I became CEO of Interstellar, he became the head of research and development, not because of me, but because of our work on the project that had pushed us together. We had a common goal—a new engine technology that would revolutionize the industry, and we were so close.

I knew that, as a company, we needed him, even if I didn't want a damn thing to do with him.

He had a brilliant mind, and Interstellar needed him just as much as they needed me. We were trapped together in a symbiotic relationship, even though it was toxic. He needed me to back his projects and give him free rein, while I needed him to create something so magnificent it would make Interstellar the leader in the aerospace industry and allow me to leave my mark on the universe. Like it or not, our lives were intertwined.

He pulled off the impossible, creating something that would solidify Interstellar's dominance over the entire industry.

Maybe he wasn't my biggest mistake after all.

Chapter 1

Trent sits down, his straight brown hair wild and messy, fitting his mad scientist persona to a T. He places his hands behind his head and kicks back in the chair. "How much do you love me?"

I take a deep breath and count to three. I'm not in the mood for his flirtatious banter this early in the morning. But then again, I never am. "We've been over this before. You need to knock before entering my office. Strolling in like you own the place is not acceptable."

Trent never did fully grasp the boundaries I'd put in place after we broke up. Being the CEO and his boss hasn't earned me an ounce of respect in his eyes either. He comes and goes as he pleases, no matter how many times I've reminded him he can't just breeze into my office like we're still a couple.

"Come on, Lulu." He gives me the classic Trent "I'm the man" chin lift.

I hate when he calls me Lulu. He gave me the nickname a few months after we started dating, and it always gave me the creeps. For being such a brilliant man, at times, he's completely clueless.

"What do you want?" I try to keep the anger from my voice, but I fail miserably.

He shows off the dimple that I used to adore but now despise. "You lost your sparkle, sweetheart. What's wrong?"

I rise from my chair, stroll to the front of my desk, and lean against it. "Skip the bullshit, Trent. It's not going to work on me anymore." Crossing my arms, I stare down at the man I once thought I loved. "What's wrong with the design?"

He smiles smugly. "Nothing. It's perfect."

It's hard to imagine a time when I believed Trent was charming, but I fell for him hook, line, and sinker.

My mouth falls open, and my arms drop. "It's done?"

That damn dimple deepens. "Yep."

"You did it?" I whisper, gripping the edge of my desk, unable to believe what he's telling me.

I shouldn't be shocked that he found a way to make the engine work. It's the reason I never fired him. Trent isn't just a genius; he has the ability to rank right up there with Albert Einstein if he's only given a chance.

He squares his shoulders and puffs out his chest, because Trent wouldn't be Trent without his cockiness. "I did."

"Do you know what this means?"

The enormity of this moment isn't lost on me.

My heart beats wildly as my mind reels from the news.

He did it.

We did it.

Interstellar pulled off something no one ever thought possible, and Trent made it happen. Suddenly, I'm thankful I never fired him even if he's a daily pain in my ass. I'm all about taking one for the team, especially when they come through in a big way.

He stands and invades my personal space with his aquamarine eyes gazing into mine. "That I'm a legend." He moves closer, and I lean backward, trying to put more space between us. "Bound to be remembered for eternity."

He cages me in, but in this moment, I'm not angry. How can I be after he just delivered the most amazing news? "Yeah, Trent, you will." It's true and ridiculous all at once. "But this means that we're going to crush the bastards at Cozza."

"It's what you always wanted." He starts to stroke the exposed skin on my arm. "We make an amazing team, Lauren."

Team? We haven't been a team in years, and even then, we were two entities that spent time together but didn't gel as one. I was too busy busting my ass to climb the corporate ladder, and Trent, well, his brilliant mind never seemed to stay focused long enough. When we were a couple, he never paid as much attention to me as he does now.

The man doesn't understand boundaries. Not only does he breeze into my office whenever he feels like it, but he touches me more than I'd like. By that I mean, if he touches me once, it's too much. But I can't knee him in the balls in my office. Even if he doesn't act professionally, I must.

I dig my fingernails into the wood on the underside of my desk, and I narrow my eyes. I grit my teeth, but keep my voice down so the rest of the office doesn't overhear. "Get your hands off me."

His thumb brushes against my flesh, too close to my breast as he ignores my request. "The new engine is my gift to you. Someday, you'll come back to me."

"Trent." I finally duck under his arm and move behind my desk again. I grip the back of my chair and raise my chin. "I appreciate the thoughtfulness behind your accomplishment, but there will never be an us again."

"I'll wait for you. Bask in the knowledge that it's ready for the final test phase before we can launch it into production, Lulu."

I wrinkle my nose and tamp down a growl that's building in the back of my throat. "Thanks." My tone is clipped and cold. "I look forward to reading your report and bringing it before the board for final approval. Can you have it on my desk before the end of the day?"

"Already done. Cassie has it."

I'm at a loss for words.

Trent's always been thorough but not when it comes to paperwork. The man could build anything with his hands, but ask him to write something down, and he becomes inarticulate and lazy.

I clear my throat. "I'll call an emergency meeting and get the ball rolling ASAP."

He turns to face me before he makes it to the door. "Want to have a drink with me after work to celebrate?"

"It's never going to happen, Trent. We have a business relationship, and that's it."

"But..."

I hold up my hand because I don't want to waste another minute having this useless, repetitive conversation. "Trent, stop making a fool of yourself."

I swear I hear him mumble bitch as he walks out, but I don't say anything because I don't want to give him a reason to come back.

Before I can sit, Cassie strides into the room holding Trent's report. "Thank God he's gone."

"Tell me about it," I mumble and hold out my hand, eager to read about the new engine. "Let me see that."

She places the report in my hands. "I'm sorry he just walked in. I tried to stop him." Her lips are pursed as she speaks, but I've told her a hundred times I never blame her for his intrusion.

"Don't worry about it."

She sinks into the chair Trent just occupied and kicks off her high heels. "Is there anything you need me to do right now?"

Cassie's been my assistant and lifeline for the last five years. She's always prompt and put together, dedicated to her job and to me, and I don't know if I could do my job without her by my side.

Typically, she knows what I want and need before I do, but she also knows the report Trent has placed in her hands, ones I trust implicitly, is important to the future of the company and will consume my entire morning.

I open the report and push down on the spine with my index finger as my eyes start sweeping over the first paragraph. "Can you call an emergency board meeting for tomorrow morning at nine?"

"On it," she says before leaving.

I sit for the next hour, reading word-by-word in complete awe. Most of the information has been so under wraps, even I didn't know everything until now.

The cocky bastard had figured out a way to make the engine work without using jet or rocket fuel. No longer would we be the second-largest aerospace company in the world, we were going to rule the universe.

Interstellar is about to become the leader in travel. Not just airline travel, but his invention could be used to power ships into outer space and allow humans to travel farther than they'd ever gone before.

This is a game changer.

I'm one step closer to achieving my dream and my father's.

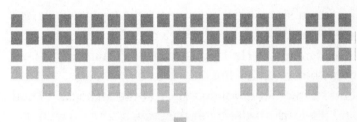

Chapter 2

In under one hour, I'll be presenting the proposal to the board members to get the go-ahead on the final testing phase of the new engine. Without their consent and their willingness to spend almost a billion dollars, we'd remain number two.

But I had Trent's plan, my vision, and a real chance to do something civilization had never achieved... reaching the outer edges of our solar system without using rocket fuel.

I'm about to place the final proposal on the table when Josh Goldman stalks into the boardroom. "We have a problem." He's almost hyperventilating as he clutches his chest.

My hand freezes a few inches above the table. "What's wrong?"

The nervous excitement I felt immediately morphs into nausea deep in the pit of my stomach.

Josh runs his fingers through his dirty-blond hair and looks over his shoulder, peering into the hallways before answering. "It's Cozza. Dawn raid. The bastards," he says, stammering out the words and not talking in complete sentences.

Josh is my number two at Interstellar. He started a few months after I did with a nose for business and a love of numbers. He's usually calm and collected, though today he's anything but.

I slowly sit down and stare at the mahogany wood and the intricate design of the grain as I try to wrap my head around the information.

As with other dawn raids, Cozza purchased a minority stake in Interstellar just as the markets opened this morning. They are positioning themselves for a takeover.

It was old-school, sneaky, and purely Cozza, the cocky bastards. It was their way of making their intentions public to take over Interstellar without a huge media splash. Dawn raids were rare, especially in the United States, but I should've known Cozza would try anything to stop us. This meant only one thing—they've officially declared war, and somehow, they knew about the engine.

"Do you know what this means?" Josh collapses in the chair next to me.

Swallowing down the lump that's settled in my throat, I nod. "I do."

I don't want to believe it, but I should've known they'd pull something like this on the verge of our announcement. The timing's uncanny and screams foul play, but things like this happen all the time in our industry... I should've expected it.

"They're going to try to take us over, Lauren."

"It won't happen," I say with a firm voice, trying to make myself believe the words as I speak them.

Josh mashes his hands together tightly, and there's a vein bulging from his forehead. "How can you be so sure?"

Tapping my fingernail against the conference table, I look out the window and try to think of a good answer. "I don't know, Josh, but we better get every goddamn person on finding a way to stop Cozza dead in their tracks."

This news changes everything.

No longer is this a meeting to discuss the exciting future of Interstellar, but the focus now shifts to how to save Interstellar and stop the slow bleed of shares to Cozza.

The stockholders need to know to hold their shares and not sell them under any circumstances. No matter what Cozza offers, with the invention just on the horizon, they'd be wealthier than they ever imagined.

He rises from his chair and fists his hands at his sides. "I'll get the junior executives on it."

Based on his anxiety, I can be certain Josh isn't behind the information leak that led Cozza to purchase the stock overnight.

But if not him, who?

There aren't many people who know about the engine outside of the design team and the top executives. The board probably had an inkling that something big was happening since we called an emergency board meeting, but I can't imagine they'd shoot themselves in the foot...especially when it came to money.

"Wait." My voice is surprisingly calm and unwavering as I speak. "Don't."

He stops and turns. "Why?"

"We don't want word getting out until the board of directors knows about Cozza's intentions. As soon as the meeting is over, we'll put everyone on it."

His Adam's apple bobs and he nods, closing his eyes briefly. "Fine." He looks down at his watch. "We have one hour before everyone gets here. We'd better come up with a way to break the news gently."

"We'll start with the original agenda. We'll rave about the invention and needing final approval for the test phase so we can begin production as soon as possible. After we have everyone excited, we'll drop the news about Cozza. With the revelation that we're about to become the leader and make everyone in the room filthy rich, they'll work their asses off to come up with a solution to get rid of Cozza and secure the corporation."

He pulls on the cuffs of his dress shirt before straightening his tie. "If you think that's a good idea."

Josh rarely goes against me, but he isn't sold on my plan either. Although he'd love to have my job, Interstellar means just as much to him as it does me. We both gave our blood, sweat, and tears to this company, and neither of us wants it to be for nothing.

"It's the only way to go."

"You're right."

Standing near the floor-to-ceiling glass windows of the conference room, I stare at the bustling city below after Josh leaves. There's no way in hell I'm going to allow years of work to be stolen by Cozza and their infamous CEO, Antonio Forte.

Little is known about the man, the myth, the legend that is Mr. Forte. Since he was appointed head of Cozza International, he's become somewhat of a recluse—at least when it comes to public events and cameras. The one thing I know about him is that he is a vulture. Most likely, he's a portly old man, sitting alone in a dark room with nothing else to do but prey on the weaker companies surrounding his precious Cozza. He's knocked off competition over the years without an ounce of remorse, and I vowed that would never happen to us.

Even if Josh has reservations about leading with the original agenda, it's the right plan. As the minutes tick by and the board members enter the room, my anxiety heightens.

Interstellar board members' sole purpose is to look out for the interest of the shareholders, which number in the millions. We have five board members, and each has very different agendas, but they all have the best interest of the company at heart.

Mr. Grayson is the first to enter, as is always the case. The older gentleman wouldn't know how to be late if his life depended on it. "Nice to see you, dear." He greets me the same every time, giving me a handshake and a wink. If anyone else would refer to me as "dear," I probably would take offense, but when Grayson says it, I kind of melt a bit. Maybe it is the fact that he reminds me more of a grandfather or my father, whom I miss so terribly that I embrace the term of endearment.

Next in the room is the cold and often calculating Ms. Edwards. Mr. Edwards, her ex-husband, used to run Interstellar, but after a very embarrassing scandal that dealt with his treatment of women at the company, not only did he step down, but his wife took him to the cleaners. I clapped for her...silently, of course. But she didn't let what her husband did keep her down. After she took his shares of the company, she walked into Interstellar like she owned the place. With the amount of shares she held, she practically did.

As the others arrive, my hearing becomes more acute, listening to the murmuring of the people in the room as they speak. I shake hands and greet everyone before I make my way to the head of the table. All the while, I never stop thinking of a way to stop the impending takeover.

When all board members have been seated, I clear my throat and wait for the galley to quiet down. "Ladies and gentlemen." I pause for their complete attention before continuing. "You're here today to approve the final phase of our newest invention. The engineering team has finalized an engine that does not require fuel of any sort and is ready for testing before we begin production."

Murmurs start, members turning to the person sitting at their side, all talking quietly with smiles on their faces. I hear the word amazing more than once.

Pacing behind their chairs, I watch them closely. Is the traitor among them? I can't imagine that's possible since this is the first they're hearing that the project is ready to move forward. "If you'd open the packet in front of you, there is information on how the engine works and the findings the design team have been able to verify through their tests thus far."

I walk around the room quietly as they read the packet that has been prepared for them, studying each person's face for any sign of betrayal because in my mind, everyone is a suspect. The voices grow louder, and the excitement becomes tangible.

"This is truly spectacular, Ms. Bradley," Mr. Grayson states.

As the longest serving member of the board, he's been too loyal to Interstellar to sell us out.

I smile. "Thank you, sir."

"How exactly does the engine work?" the newest member of the board, Mr. Connors, asks and instantly piques my curiosity.

I never liked Tad Connors. He always has a question, and there's something about him that keeps me on edge. Maybe it's the way his eyes linger a little too long on my legs when I wear a skirt or his perpetual quest to find out the exact information I'd never reveal.

"I can't divulge that information. The patent is still pending, and leaking the details, even to the board, wouldn't be in the best interest of Interstellar."

He runs his hand backward against his hair, making sure every strand is perfectly slicked back. "Understood."

"All I can say is that it will change the aerospace industry forever. Imagine being able to reach Mars without an ounce of rocket fuel to power the vehicle. Or flying to Europe without hundreds of gallons of jet fuel to pollute the environment."

"Astonishing." Tad relaxes back in the high-back leather chair, watching me closely as I pace the length of the room.

But today, I wore pants to keep his eyes on the prize instead of my calves.

"If we approve the final testing today, production can be started in under three months, and the first Interstellar engine can be in the air in well under a year."

"That soon?" Ms. Edwards's perfectly plucked black eyebrows shoot up before a small grin spreads across her thin red lips.

"Yes, ma'am. There's nothing stopping us once we prove the design is safe and reliable."

"How certain are we of that the test will work?" Mr. Jameson asks before I can say another word.

In his mid-sixties and extremely wealthy, along with being drop-dead gorgeous for a silver fox, he isn't in it for the money. He believes in the company and our dreams for the future. Mainly he's driven by the dreams of his children. His oldest, Bennett, is in the Air Force with hopes of entering the space program someday.

"Based on the initial test data, the work of the design team, and the report on my desk, I'd say that I'm fairly confident the engine will work as planned without an issue." Returning to my spot at the head of the table, I pray I won't have to eat my words.

Ms. Kirby, the member with a legal background who always seems to worry about the legalities more than our legal department, pipes in before I can put it to a vote. "So, by doing the test, we're announcing to the world the new project. Has Interstellar taken the necessary steps to patent the invention and keep as much detail from leaking into the wrong hands? We want to maximize the potential growth for Interstellar and their stockholders, along with protecting the future assets of the company."

I want to growl as a warning for her to back off. The entire company has been working on the project in some form, and we did everything possible. "Yes, Ms. Kirby, we have taken the necessary steps, including patenting the technology." There is no time to waste and more business to discuss, which will hit on Ms. Kirby's second part of the question. "Let's vote. All in favor."

One by one, I count the raised hands around the table even though everyone has theirs in the air. A unanimous decision is exactly what I had expected when I called the meeting yesterday.

"It's unanimous. The final step in testing will be scheduled. I'll send a memo when we have a date for members to attend."

Before I can continue, Mr. Grayson starts to push back from the table. "Thank you." He stands, and all members start to follow suit.

"We have one other item to discuss."

Mr. Grayson turns toward me, his eyebrows turned inward when his eyes meet mine.

"This morning something came to my attention." The twelve sets of eyes around the table are glued to me. I clear my throat, looking above them for a moment. The room becomes silent, almost deafening.

In all the board meetings, I'd presided over, never had I introduced something not on the original agenda. "Cozza International purchased a minority stake in Interstellar this morning. As you all know, Cozza is our main competitor. Based on this information, I'm expecting an announcement soon about their plan to take over Interstellar. I feel that by their purchasing the stake in the company, it's in our best interest to speed up the engine testing to help boost the price of the stock and stave off any further stock grabs by Cozza."

"How can this be?" Mr. Grayson slams his fist down on the conference table, acting out in a way I'd never expected.

The murmurs of excitement from earlier now change to panic. "Ladies and gentlemen of the board," I call out, trying to gain control of the room, but I keep my voice even. "We need to work together, along with the executive team, to find a way to stop Cozza from taking possession of Interstellar. I find it unsettling that their takeover attempt falls on the heels of our newest breakthrough, but we must forge on and do everything in our power to stop them. We need to make sure they are not able to purchase any more stock in Interstellar and do everything in our power to stop their advances."

"How?" Ms. Edwards asks while nervously stroking her neck.

"There has to be a way to stop them. If you're approached by anyone from Cozza, it's imperative that you don't speak with them and under no circumstances sell them your shares. They need to purchase a majority stake in the company in order to complete their takeover. The legal team, in conjunction with other executives, will be formulating a plan to halt them in their tracks and put the takeover to bed."

"Forte has stooped to a new low," Mr. Grayson says through gritted teeth, the wrinkles around his eyes growing deeper. "Cozza tried this years ago and were unsuccessful. I'm sure they'll be stopped this time, too." Even though he speaks the words, I don't feel the conviction in his voice.

I grip the back of my chair and dig my fingernails into the soft leather. "I'll keep everyone updated on our progress, and we'll be working around the clock to find a solution."

Tad stands and rubs the back of his neck. "Do we know who the mole is?"

"We don't," I inform the group, even though the list has grown shorter as the meeting went on. There's too much money to be made for them to sell out Interstellar and share our secrets with the competition. That only leaves a member of the design team as the sellout. "It doesn't matter. All that matters now is that we stop them."

"Exactly," Josh states, finally adding to the conversation and coming to stand at my side. "Rest assured this is our first priority."

I lean into his space. "Finally," I whisper without moving my lips.

He keeps his eyes pinned to the board members. "I'll always have your back," he whispers back to me.

"Let's adjourn so that we may get started on finding a solution as soon as possible," I announce, walking away from Josh and heading toward the door to shake the board members' hands as they exit.

"Let me know if I can be of help," Ms. Edwards says with a small smile before strutting down the hallway in her knee-high Louboutin boots and skintight black skirt.

"Bradley." Tad stops in front of me, catching my attention. "When you find the mole, you cut him off at the knees. We're too close to something amazing and world-changing to allow the credit to go to Cozza."

"Agreed." I stare into his eyes.

He couldn't be the one.

He's too money hungry and knows what the invention would mean for his bottom line.

"I'll do what's necessary, Tad." I smile and hold my breath until he walks out.

"Lauren." Mr. Grayson shakes my hand. "You have my entire legal team at your service. I've been with Interstellar too long to allow Cozza to take the credit for all your hard work. We're too close to something that will revolutionize the entire industry."

"I know, Mr. Grayson." I study his aged face.

The deep wrinkles near his dark brown eyes give him character and make him appear kinder than everyone knows him to be. The man's a pit bull and would take out any enemy that got in his way.

"I promise to protect Interstellar."

He pats the top of my hand. "Thank you, dear."

I give his hand a small squeeze before he walks out and I turn to find an empty boardroom. Standing here, I close my eyes and give myself exactly five seconds to let fear seep inside. Just enough time to allow it to finally hit home. I count to five and then head straight to my office to start to deal with Cozza.

As I shut my office door, I lean against it. The enormity of what's transpired is enough to crush me. How could this possibly be happening? I thought I had done everything in my power to surround myself with the best people—the most loyal, most driven. But there is a hole somewhere. Why now? It's too close to the engine development to be coincidence. This is calculated and led by someone in-house who spilled the news of the design to our competition. When everything seemed to be clicking into place, the bottom dropped out, and now I must do everything in my power to fix it.

I push off the door and head toward my desk to devise a plan, one which starts with my VP. "Cassie, get Josh in here and take messages on any calls today. We're not to be disturbed."

"Yes, ma'am," Cassie replies before I disconnect the call.

I won't leave the office until I have confidence that our team has a solution.

I wouldn't go down.

Not now.

Not like this.

Not ever.

Chapter 3

Twelve hours later, I stumble out of the office, completely exhausted. My head's spinning from all the jargon and different scenarios we ran through for how to stop Cozza in its tracks.

I want a martini—scratch that, I need a martini. Probably more than even one, if I'm being honest. The W Hotel's just down the street and makes the best drinks in town. It's my go-to place when I need to unwind after a long day, and it's on my way home. The dark lighting and calming colors make it perfect to gather my thoughts and relax.

I place my order, shrug off my knee-length Michael Kors coat, and take a seat on a barstool, far from anyone else who may want to chitchat. I watch the bartender mix the martini, waiting for my first sip while my mouth salivates and I take in my exhausted features in the mirror behind the bar.

Being on top causes more stress than I could ever fully explain to another person not in my shoes. Every employee, shareholder, and board member looks to me for leadership. Who could I go to for help when there are moments that make me question my sanity?

No one.

There isn't a single person I could share my doubts, fears, or moments of madness with who wouldn't consider me weak. Not even my family would understand the weight I have on my shoulders. Therefore, I turn to the only good listener I know—vodka.

It helps take the edge off without having to spill my guts to a stranger and end up with a prescription for something that would numb my mind and make me useless as CEO. I need to stay sharp. I need to be alert to the people wanting to take me down and destroy Interstellar.

I lift the glass to my lips, inhaling the salty splendor before I take a small sip.

Heaven.

"Is this seat taken?" a man asks at my right, interrupting my moment of bliss as the second mouthful slides down my throat.

I motion toward the empty seat without a word, not bothering to look at him. The last thing I want to do is make small talk with a stranger. Talking means not drinking. Not drinking means thinking.

My mind's too much of a mess, and I need to calm the chaos inside if I'm ever going to get to sleep.

Ignoring his presence, I continue savoring each sip and stare at the picture hanging above the mirror behind the bar. It's a simple work—an aerial view of the Chicago skyline at night. Each building is lit up, standing tall and beautiful.

Everything looks unimportant from so high in the air. The people are invisible from above, the city appearing as lonely as I feel. The struggles, fears, and panic below can't be seen, but they are happening in different people's lives at the moment that photo was snapped.

I may dislike Trent and regret every moment I spent in his bed, but there's one thing I miss—being close to someone. Working with him made it easy to share the day-to-day challenges I felt while climbing the corporate ladder. He understood. But in the end, it wasn't enough to keep me at his side.

I had my martini, the bar, and an empty apartment, but no complication from a jealous boyfriend. Some things had to be put on hold in order to attain the level of success I've achieved in such a short time. Relationships often led to marriage, which led to kids. I didn't have time to devote to a family and still work to my best ability at Interstellar.

Setting my glass down, I rest my cheek on my hand and twirl the stem of the glass between my fingertips. I keep staring at the photo, wondering if I'd make a difference in the world. After my time passes, would I have created enough of an impact to make all the sacrifices worth it? What are wealth and success worth if there's no one there to savor the moment with you?

"Is it always this chilly in May?"

The sexy accent makes the hairs on my arm stand straight up as if being beckoned by the deep purr.

"Yes." I'm almost frozen in place with my hand still on my glass.

When he lifts his hands to his mouth, blowing into his palms before rubbing them together, I almost sneak a glance, but something stops me.

"I'll never get used to the cold."

"No one ever does."

He pulls his stool closer, and I catch a whiff of his expensive cologne. "Why live here, then?"

Between his scent and the sound of his voice, I know I'm a goner if he's handsome. "It's where I was born and where I'll die." Even when I went to school in Boston, I longed for the grittiness of Chicago.

"No one is ever trapped. Why not move?"

"I work here. It's where my life is, and I also love this city." I take another sip, keeping my eyes straight ahead.

He finally takes a sip of his drink. "It's beautiful for an American city."

That statement alone aggravates me. He used the word American as if it were derogatory. I've traveled all over the world in my lifetime and still hadn't found a city to rival Chicago.

Maybe Paris. Maybe.

But it still doesn't have the same grittiness of Chicago. It may be more beautiful, but it will never be home.

"What's your name?"

Finally, I turn, allowing myself to see the man who wants to interrupt the moment that my martini and I are having.

Damn it.

Naturally, he not only smells like sin and sounds like heaven, but he's drop-dead gorgeous too.

The type of man I would've welcomed into my bed if it weren't for the fact that all I wanted to do is drink. The dark brown hair around his face is windblown, light scruff on his face lining his lush lips perfectly. His light sky-blue eyes bore into me, filled with curiosity and something I hadn't planned on—lust.

"Elizabeth," I lie. I don't feel like being me, and since I don't know him, I don't want to give away more than I have to, which at this point, is nothing.

"Elizabeth," he repeats, holding out his hand to mine. Hesitantly, I slide my hand against his palm, letting his warmth transfer to my ice-cold fingers. "I'm Lou."

"Nice to meet you, Lou."

He pulls my hand to his lips and kisses the top, scorching my skin in their wake. "What brings you here tonight?"

As soon as he releases my hand from his grip, I miss his warmth. Quickly, I grab the glass between my hands, averting my eyes, and trying to cool the flesh he'd just touched. "Just a drink before I head home."

"May I buy you another?"

"Why?" I glance at him over my shoulder in confusion.

"Because I don't like to drink alone." He grabs his tumbler of Cognac. "I don't know anyone here, and I'd rather you stay for a while."

I take another sip of my martini, staring at his arms, which are bulging beneath the silk fabric. "Why me?"

The sleeves on his dress shirt are rolled up, exposing his forearms and wrists, which are masculine and thick. A smattering of hair covers his thick, corded muscles that melt into the dress shirt near his elbow, straining against the material and becoming one.

If I'm going to stay and play someone I'm not, I figure I'll need another drink to get through it. I don't know why I'm even thinking about staying. But all I have to do is look at Lou, and I know why—he's head-to-toe handsome.

But tonight, more than any other, I feel the need to get lost. I can't run away and forget everything that's happening, but I can drink and role-play, pretending to be someone else. I never let go, tossing caution to the wind, but tonight the thought's intoxicating. Tonight, I want to be anyone but me.

He looks around the bar before turning his full attention toward me. "I don't see anyone else as beautiful as you are."

I can't stop my crooked smile. "Thanks."

I shouldn't be so enamored with the compliment. There are only three other people sitting around the bar, staring at the television as the Cubs lose yet another game.

Clearly, the martini was more powerful than I anticipated. Maybe I should've eaten something before I started drinking tonight. Normally, such a small flirtation wouldn't have an impact, but between his beautiful face and smooth accent, I'm a goner.

"So, will you stay?" He points at my martini glass that's now almost empty and waits for my response.

It can't hurt to stay for one more, right?

"Sure."

"Another round," he tells the bartender, pointing down to our glasses before he strokes his chin, the stubble on his face moving underneath his fingertips. "So, what do you do, Elizabeth?"

I can't take my eyes off his face. I watch his fingers and wonder about the coarseness of his stubble and how it would feel rubbing against my skin. Would it tickle? I've never been with a man with as much hair on his face as he has. It has to be soft and my fingers itch to touch it, but I refrain. "I'm an executive assistant."

If I'm going to lie, which I am, why not go big? People rarely have questions for assistants. If I mention the word CEO, we'd sit here and talk about my career, and it's the one thing I want to avoid.

"Do you love it?" He tilts his head back before his eyes search my face.

"I do. What do you do?" I need to deflect and move on before I change my mind and leave.

He smiles, revealing his perfectly white, straight teeth. "I'm a pilot."

I drag my eyes to his and realize he caught me staring at his mouth. It's been ages since I've had sex. Trent was my last, and that was eons ago. Being this close to a man, a handsome one at that, with the vodka buzzing through my system has my mind wandering. His spicy cologne isn't helping the matter either. "That sounds exciting." Images of the mile-high club start to fill my brain—dirty bits of him and how he sounds when he moans—in his pilot's uniform and aviator sunglasses.

When the bartender sets the drinks down, Lou slides the martini in front of me, brushing against my arm and bringing me back to reality. "It can be," he says.

I'd been so busy earlier trying to avoid him, that I hadn't fully appreciated how different he smells. The cologne he wears is expensive and not common. "I'm sorry if I was cold when you sat down."

His smile reaches his large blue eyes. "I wouldn't say that."

I finally let myself relax, wrapping my fingers around my glass. I move it in circles and watch the liquid slosh around. "I've had such a bad day."

"What can I do to make it better?"

I look over at him as he winks, and my cheeks instantly heat, the flush creeping up my neck to meet the redness in my face. "Just this." I motion between us and try to steady my breathing.

Being this close to a man has never affected me. But the dull ache between my thighs when he looks at me and the way he licks his lips has my body reeling. Maybe it's the amount of stress I'm under today or quite possibly the drink I just had on an empty stomach. Either way, I crave his touch.

His tongue pokes out, sweeping across his bottom lip before he speaks. "You want to talk about it?"

I shake my head slowly and stare at his mouth, wondering how he tastes. "I just want to drink and think about something else."

"Personal life or work?"

"Work." I sigh, dragging my eyes away to stare down at my drink.

"Ah. I understand that sometimes work can be stressful, but you shouldn't let it ruin your night." There's a small crinkle in the corner of his eye, betraying his age or maybe that his life is just as stressful as mine, but it's sexy. Men can pull it off, and Lou certainly does more than that.

I finger the stem of the glass and avoid eye contact. I feel like a scumbag lying to him about myself. "I wish it were that easy."

He moves his lips close to my ear and speaks in a deep, husky voice. "I can help make your night better."

Shivers run down my spine as he speaks. I turn, and my mouth is inches from his. "I'm not sleeping with you." But I want to...more than anything, I want him. Drown myself in sin, lose my thought in his touch, and forget who I am for a night. I want the passion, the pleasure, and everything Lou has to offer.

He places a hand on his chest and smirks. "Elizabeth, what kind of man do you think I am?"

I smile and let my eyes travel the length of him before answering. "You look like the type of man who thinks if he buys a drink, a woman will throw herself at him." Because from the looks of him, I'm sure he never has to ask for sex. A drop-dead gorgeous man with his sexy-chic hair and lush lips probably doesn't have to anything more than smile for panties to start dropping.

"The thought never crossed my mind." He looks at me the same way I just looked at him. "You definitely don't look like the type to sleep with a random stranger."

"I'm not," I shoot back, but I feel my face flush. I've never been the type to do the walk of shame, but a man like Lou could tempt me under different circumstances. "As long as we're clear."

"Crystal."

I lied.

Two martinis later, making a total of three, and I've changed my mind. I want to sleep with Lou.

Sleep? No. No.

I want to fuck Lou.

He spent the last hour regaling me with his travels and the joy of being a pilot. The way he spoke about it made it seem like the most freeing job in the world. To soar above the clouds, the world silent below, sounds magical.

"Lou," I whisper against the rim of the martini glass with one hand resting on his forearm. "Will you take me flying sometime?"

Being with him has been easy. I didn't have to think about my job or worry about anything. I could just listen and stare at his handsome ruggedness without a thought other than him. I glance down at my hand and realize I've been touching him for most of the conversation with my fingers resting on his forearm.

"You name the time and place." His deep voice sounds as smooth as the liquor in the back of my throat.

"How long are you in town?"

Why did I ask him that?

There's no way I can ever see him again. I can't keep pretending to be Elizabeth the executive assistant, and I have way too much on my plate right now for frivolous fun.

"For a little while."

"A week?"

"Probably more."

"I get the hint." I push my empty glass forward.

"Hey." He moves closer to me, and I feel his warmth as he rests his hand on my knee. "I'm not blowing you off. I'm here for training, and it can take a while for me to finish. It depends on my schedule."

I give him a weak smile. "It doesn't matter, Lou. I'm too busy with work to fly away with you." I really didn't even have the time to sit here and have drinks with him either, but here I am, sitting, drinking, and flirting like I don't have a care in the world.

His fingers softly stroke the inside of my knee, and my breath hitches, causing goose bumps to break out across my skin. "Can I take you to dinner tomorrow night?"

"I can't," I say, my voice breathy and betraying.

"The next night."

I grimace. "Sorry, but I just can't."

"You pretend you don't want me, Liz, but I can tell you do. The way your breathing changes when I do this." His fingers inch higher up my leg, and I regret that I wore pants today as he makes tiny circles against my flesh. "I can tell that you want me. The way your eyes dilate when I get closer or you stare at my mouth." He licks his lips, and I follow the path of his tongue. "You know you want me. Admit it." By the time he stops speaking, my fingernails are digging into the skin of his arm.

My body says yes, but my brain tells me to walk away—at least the part that's still sober. The insanely hot man in the expensive dress shirt with his sleeves rolled up, wearing tailored black dress pants he fills out nicely, and a face so handsome he could grace the cover of GQ, wants me. How am I supposed to say no?

Tomorrow, I'll go back to reality, but there's always tonight.

"I'm attracted to you." Admitting it isn't easy for me, but I have liquid courage. Maybe it's more stupidity, but I say the words before I can change my mind.

He brings his face closer to mine. "Then spend the night with me," he whispers.

One-night stands have never been my thing. I've done them just like every other red-blooded American, but it wasn't the reason I came here tonight. I needed to get lost and forget about everything. Lou gave me that out. The conversation alone did the trick, along with the three martinis I drank. But the thought of seeing him naked makes my mouth salivate and my spine tingle.

I swallow down my fear and lead with my body instead of my mind. "Okay."

He flattens his hand on my leg before curling it around my thigh. "Come on." He reaches into his pocket with his free hand, pulling out a money clip before tossing some bills on the bar.

I think about changing my mind, but then his fingers start to move, and all doubt vanishes. "Are you staying here?"

He holds out his hand to me, waiting for me to take it and seal the deal. "Yes."

Clearly, the stress of the day must've had a greater effect than I thought. After three martinis and a lot of flirting, it doesn't matter—I want him.

I grab my purse from the bar and turn to face him, a devilish smile on my face while my insides are doing backflips.

"Are you sure?" he asks when I put my hand in his.

My smile may be cockeyed, probably from the drinks, but my answer is clear and direct. I climb off the stool and smooth my shirt with one free hand. "Yes. Are you?"

He wraps his arm around my back and steadies me as we walk out of the hotel bar. The spark between us is almost visible as we steal glances at each other, walking through the lobby. My need grows stronger the closer we get to the elevators, and the butterflies inside my stomach are flying around with excitement.

By the time we make it to the elevator bank, I don't feel as tipsy as I did when I agreed to go to his room. "Elizabeth," he says, pulling my body closer to his. "I need to know that you want this. I don't take advantage of women." His fingers tighten on my waist. "I want you. More than anything, I want to taste you."

I peer into his eyes. "I want you, Lou."

Chapter 4

As soon as the elevator doors open, he whisks me inside and presses the button behind my back. Before I can move, he has me against the wall, and his lips are on mine. He tastes like sweet Cognac when his tongue sweeps inside my mouth. I moan, wanting more of him as my fingers find their way into his thick, dark hair.

His hand slides up my leg, brushing the edge of my panties underneath my dress pants, and my knees go weak. The kissing's frantic. Consuming. The only sounds besides the beeping at each floor are our rushed breaths, my moans, and his grunts. With each passing floor, the need grows and the kissing becomes more frenzied.

By the time the doors open, he has my top unbuttoned, and I've untucked his shirt and slipped my fingers underneath. We tumble out of the doors at the penthouse, stripping each other bare as we walk. When the backs of my knees hit the couch, I topple backward, and his hard body lands on top of mine without breaking our kiss.

"Lou," I moan into his mouth, dragging my nails against his scalp.

"Elizabeth," he groans before kissing me deeper. Harder.

My lips are bruised and already swollen, but I don't want him to stop. Overcome with need, I wrap my legs around his body and lock my ankles to keep him flush against me. It's been so long since I'd been with someone that I almost forget how good it feels to be underneath a man and consumed by his weight.

Lou kisses me like the very air he breathes depends on it. His tongue sweeps inside my mouth, chasing mine, and nipping at my lips here and there. Fuck, the man feels fantastic, and his kissing skills are off the charts. Not sloppy at all, with the perfect amount of tongue and teeth to make everything inside my body flutter with excitement.

When he starts to slide down my body, I loosen my legs and give him free rein to do whatever he wants. I want to feel him everywhere against my skin. Instead of closing my eyes, I watch his every movement, completely enthralled by his handsomeness and the hungriness in his eyes.

He hovers over my nipple, his warm breath cascading across my skin and making it pebble into a stiff peak. It's like it wants to leap into his mouth, sick of being trapped and lonely underneath my stiff business suit. Lou's mouth is warm and inviting, and my body wants everything he has to offer.

I jolt, my back rising off the couch as his mouth closes around my nipple. "Fuck," I hiss as my eyes close to revel in the ecstasy only his mouth could create. His blue eyes watch me, burning into mine as he sucks on the peak and causing me to squirm.

His hands slide up my body and push my arms over my head. Unable to move with his weight and his arms pinning mine, I give in to his wants. I try not to think about anything but the feel of him on me, forcing my entire life out of my mind.

Tonight, I'm Elizabeth.

Lou wants her.

I want Lou to fuck her.

Before I can dig my fingers into his hair and drag him back up my body to tell him just how much I want to fuck him, he releases my nipple, crawling down my legs and kneeling on the floor. He rips off my pants along with my panties in one quick motion. I gasp, shocked by his abilities to divest a woman of her clothing so easily, but a guy like Lou probably has had a lot of practice.

I'm sprawled across a chaise with my feet hanging on each side of his shoulders. I glance down at him, ready to speak, when he grabs my ankles and yanks my body down, stopping when my ass hits the edge.

"Fucking perfection," he says, parting my legs wider to give him a full view.

My legs start to close on their own as my face begins to heat.

He rests his hands against my knees and keeps me from hiding. "Don't."

I feel vulnerable and exposed with his eyes taking in my nakedness at close proximity, but I do as he tells me.

His lips blaze a trail up my thighs, scorching my flesh in their wake. I flinch uncontrollably when he hits the sweet spot right behind my knee. It has always been one of the most sensitive areas on my body, and he found it rather quickly.

I can't speak. His mouth's devouring my skin, and my breathing's so harsh I can't form words. Just as I catch my breath and find my voice, he's moved to a new area, and the struggle starts all over again.

Stop thinking so much...just feel him.

My fingers wrap around the edges of the couch so tightly that my knuckles turn white. I gasp for air, clutching the cushions, and I spread my legs wider, trying to get his face to find the one spot I want.

"Do you want me to lick your pussy?" Lou's deep, hypnotic voice causes my eyes to dart to his.

"Yes," I breathe.

He licks his lips, and my eyes follow their path. "Tell me." He smirks, knowing he has me right where he wants me.

The sad thing is that he does have me by the proverbial balls. "Lick it." This time my voice has more air to it, more want in the tone.

"Put your feet on the edge and spread them, Lizzy."

My heart starts to flutter, the excitement of what is about to happen becoming almost too much. I place my body just how he wants and wait. But when nothing happens, I peer down to his smug face.

"You still haven't told me what you want me to do." His smirk grows wider.

"Lick my pussy," I tell him flat out through gritted teeth and with a firmer voice. "Then fuck me until I can't walk tomorrow, Lou. Put up or shut up, big boy."

"That's my dirty girl." He sticks two fingers in his mouth, sucking on them, and my eyes start to roll back at the thought of him doing the same thing to my clit.

"I'm waiting," I tell him, spreading my legs wider as his eyebrows shoot up.

He hovers over my clit before barely grazing it with his tongue. Shock waves fill my entire body—the sensation is overwhelming yet not enough to get me there. "More." I lift my ass, meeting his face with my pussy. Offering it to him.

He takes the hint, closing his mouth around my core and enveloping me with his warmth. I suck in a breath, consumed by the feel of him against a part of my body that hasn't been touched by a man in so long. Everything inside me tenses from the single touch, craving the orgasm that I know will make my head spin.

"Tell me again you want me," Lou says against my skin, the vibrations of his voice causing me to shiver.

"I want you to fuckin' suck my clit, Lou." Under normal circumstances, I'd probably tell him to fuck off. But after the day I had and the amount of alcohol still coursing through my system, I want nothing more than to come in his mouth and be fucked by him.

"The lady wants to come and so she shall. Many times." He smiles against my skin before closing his mouth over me again. His tongue swirls around my hard clit, adding to the suction of his mouth and driving me so close to coming that I don't think I can last more than sixty seconds. When his fingers start to rub against my opening, I almost explode.

"Yes!" I scream out, a little too overeager to be filled.

His eyes sparkle, and even though I can't see his lips, I know he smiles. Fucker.

As he pushes a finger inside, I can't stop the moan from escaping my lips. Not a nice, sweet moan of pleasure, but a feral one as if I were in heat. "More!" I cry out after I regain my composure.

His finger curls inside me, and my eyes blur from the sensation. He's found my G-spot, and I can't stop my body from shaking with each pass. "Greedy cunt," he says, working his finger in and out as I lie here with my legs falling farther apart.

I smile because I know I'm being a completely greedy woman. I know what I want and never have a problem voicing my opinion on any matter. Sex is no different. But instead of being a tease, Lou gives me everything I want and more.

A second finger joins the first, sweeping over my G-spot with every movement. My ass rises off the couch, my breathing stops, and I shatter against his mouth. Wave after wave of pleasure racks my body. It steals the air in my lungs, my ability to moan, and seizes every muscle in my body.

He doesn't stop. Every time my body convulses, he sucks harder, making each aftershock more intense than the last. By the time he releases me, I'm gasping for air, and my entire body quivers uncontrollably. Slowly, he removes his fingers, my pussy constricting around them, not willing to let go of them just yet.

"Like I said, you have a greedy cunt."

I can't laugh even though his words are true. I'm too busy trying to catch my breath from the orgasm to end all orgasms. My mind's still fuzzy and my senses dulled as I try to smile, but it's lopsided. My eyes close to stop the spinning from the lack of oxygen, and I enjoy the feeling of coming from someone other than myself.

The sound of plastic rustling makes my eyes pop open. He's ripping the condom wrapper open with his teeth. His beautiful face between my legs looks as pleased as I feel. Lifting my head, I study his body, getting my first real look. His arms flex with each movement while he rolls the condom down his cock.

The muscles of his chest are big and tight, moving under his skin as if they're trying to break free. When he stands, I take the chance to get my fill of his entire perfect body. His strong thighs meet with what can only be described as an impressive cock that looks so hard and needy that it seems ready to burst at any moment.

By the time my eyes find their way to his face, I can see the pleasure he took in watching me eye-fuck him. "You like what you see, Lizzy?"

"I do," I tell him and bite my lip. I love what I see. The man is complete and utter perfection. Not an ounce of body fat anywhere on his torso. Just taut muscles and smooth skin itching to be touched.

There are no words to be said. When I think he's going to climb onto the couch, I inch up the cushion to give him enough room to work his magic.

His hand grabs my waist and stills me. "I want you bent over the couch."

"Oh," I say, feeling my face flush at the thought.

I turn, giving him a great view of my ass, and position myself over the back of the couch. My head hangs down, and I peer at him from the side. "Like this?" I ask, wiggling my ass.

His hand comes down on my ass just right, sending a wave of pleasurable pain up my spine. "Just like that." He caresses the skin he's just touched, and I want more of it.

I bite my lip instead of telling him to smack me again. He positions himself behind me, rubbing his cock against my wetness. Between coming and the amount of need I still have, I'm practically dripping.

When he starts to push inside, my head falls forward, and I moan. His fingers are one thing, but the hardness and size of his dick are quite another. Feeling filled by his cock makes my body ache to be filled deeper, harder, and forever. My heart thumps against my chest, trying to keep up with my erratic breathing. After he slams into me, seating himself fully, I moan from pleasure and rock back into him, forcing him deeper.

His fingers twist in my hair, pulling my head backward and trapping me. "I fuck you, not the other way around. Got me?"

Goose bumps form across my body. The dirtiness of his words and the authoritative tone of his voice have me screaming out, "Yes!"

He holds my hair, pulling me against him with every thrust of his cock. I cry out every time his dick impales me. I've never felt so full in my entire life. Pleasure courses through my system, overtaking every thought I had and wiping it away.

I'm consumed by him. Nothing else in the world matters except Lou and his spectacular cock. He controls me, and I let him. Every time his hand comes down on my ass, I cry out. "More," I tell him, which earns me a deeper thrust.

It isn't punishment. Maybe he thinks it is due to the noises coming from my mouth, but there's nothing but pleasure. Lou knows how to handle me. I never have liked being controlled, but when he does it, I want it.

Before I can stop it, a second orgasm builds inside me and tears through my body. I grip the back of the couch, gasping for air and shaking under his touch.

"Such a greedy girl," he whispers in my ear, but I can't respond. My mouth falls open and I try to form words, but nothing comes out.

I think he'll ease up. But instead, his thrusts become more punishing, almost to the point of pain. He pummels my body and releases my hair. I watch over my shoulder as his abdomen contracts with each movement. It's like a work of art or a well-oiled machine the way his body moves. When his mouth falls open and his eyes close, I know he's experiencing the same thing I just felt. Complete and total ecstasy.

He cries out, "Liz!"

For a moment, I feel guilty that he's calling out a name other than my own, but it quickly passes. Lou and I are nothing more than a cheap fling started in a hotel bar and finished on the couch in his rented room.

When his body collapses on top of me, we both tumble to the floor. We laugh at the silliness, barely missing the coffee table in our fall. "Fuck, baby. Who knew you had that in you?" Lou wraps his arm around me and brings my body flush against his.

"I could say the same about you." I giggle, burying my face in his pec.

We lie here, staring at the ceiling, gasping for air until I pass out from exhaustion.

■ ■ ■ ■ ■ ■ ■ ■

I blink, momentarily confused as I open my eyes in a bedroom I don't recognize. I blink again, and memories of last night start to come flooding back. Lou. Nakedness. Elizabeth. Sex. Sweat. Orgasms. Bliss.

What in the hell was I thinking?

Clearly, I wasn't, or I wouldn't be naked and in a stranger's bed.

The martinis clouded my judgment. It's the only thing I can blame besides myself and Lou's smooth-talking charm and accent.

I roll to the side and groan. "I'm so stupid," I whisper into the pillow. I prop myself up on my elbows because of a crinkling sound underneath my cheek. It's a note, which I assume Lou left because if it were the maid, it would be even more awkward.

Thanks for the night. I have an early plane and didn't want to wake you. - Lou

I flip it over, hoping to see his phone number, but there's nothing. I'd be lying if I didn't say I'm hurt. Even though I didn't think I'd see him again, I would've at least liked to thank him for the amazing night. How ridiculous. Thank him for the fucking? After I find my pride and give myself a little pep talk, I dress quickly, tossing Lou's note in the trash next to the bed and head home.

Chapter 5

I have just enough time to change my clothes and make it to work without being late. Inside, my heart's pounding, but on the outside, I appear calm, cool, and collected as I stride through the double glass doors of Interstellar.

"Have we found a remedy?" I ask, walking into the boardroom after throwing my things haphazardly on the couch in my office.

"The legal team has been working around the clock in shifts. Cozza's team called and wanted to set up a meeting. They're on their way here to discuss things." Josh's voice sounds like he's having a casual conversation, not holding the life of our company in his hands.

"Now?" I pinch the bridge of my nose, trying to rub away the migraine I can feel building behind my eyes.

Josh nods and begins to tap his pen against the pad of paper sitting on the conference table. "Yes."

My eyes are glued to his annoying habit, feeling each tap inside my head. I need to find aspirin if I'm going to deal with Cozza today and the pile of shit that's about to hit the fan.

"They realized that our members will fight the takeover and want to discuss a merger."

Ignoring Josh, I hit the intercom button on the phone. "Cassie."

"Yes, ma'am?"

"Can you bring me some aspirin, please?"

"Yes. Be there shortly."

Josh smirks like he can read my mind. "Have a rough night?"

"It's just a stress headache, Josh." I lie my ass off. The last thing I need is to show weakness or be judged by a male executive—especially him.

If Josh went out and had a one-night stand, people would slap him on the back and tell him he was "the man." That's the rub of the entire situation. Women, even myself, aren't given as much leeway when it comes to our sexual exploits. I didn't give a shit what he thought of me, but I didn't want to deal with the bullshit on the back of Cozza. "Why aren't you as stressed out as I am, Josh?"

His head snaps back, and his eyes narrow, zooming in on me. "What are you insinuating, Lauren?"

I wave my hand, trying to play it off as an innocent observation even though he could very well be my prime suspect. "I'm just wondering why you're so calm. I wasn't insinuating anything."

"I'm not a rat, if that's what you're thinking." His voice is stern, and his nostrils flare.

I hold up my hands to wipe all doubt from my face. "I believe you."

His face softens, and he gives me a quick nod as he pulls out a piece of paper from under his notepad. "Here's the Cozza press release that was sent out this morning."

Cozza International announces the recent acquisition of a minority stake in Interstellar Corp. Cozza has always been the leader in the aerospace industry, and a future acquisition of Interstellar will ensure the future of both companies in dominating and revolutionizing the global and international space transit market. We look forward to becoming one corporation with the same goal in mind–economic and environmentally friendly solutions to travel throughout the universe. The terms of this agreement will be disclosed shortly after both parties agree to the merger. CEO Antonio Forte says, "We look forward to working with the members of Interstellar to propel our companies into the future."

I close my eyes and take a few deep breaths. "What a load of crap. This—" I push the paper away in disgust. "This makes it sound like we want this. They're trying to take us over through hostile means. We didn't ask for this nonsense."

Josh pulls the paper back and crumples the edges under his fingertips. "I know, Lauren. It's bullshit. We'll stop them before this press release can become a reality."

"It never will be," I grumble under my breath when Cassie's voice comes through the intercom.

"Ms. Bradley."

"Yes?"

"The gentlemen from Cozza are here."

"Have them wait."

"Yes, ma'am."

"Why would you do that?" Josh asks with wide eyes.

My smile grows wider from the pleasure I feel knowing they're waiting. "Because I can."

He laughs, nodding while he covers his mouth. "Fair enough."

I lean back, relaxing into the chair and wishing I'd received the aspirin I asked for earlier. "You gather the troops, and I'll head to the lobby and welcome the Cozza reps."

"We'll be in here before you get back." Josh disappears into the hallway, heading toward the executive office area. Nothing will be discussed without them. Their fate is just as tied to the outcome of this meeting as mine.

I check my email, letting some time go by because I figure our "guests" can wait and stew. They're on my clock now. Since their advance on us is unwanted, I'll make it as uncomfortable as possible. They have us on the edge of our seats, and I'm more than happy to waste their time.

They want to take what doesn't belong to them. Interstellar isn't for sale. I'll protect it like a mother bear protecting her cub and use any means necessary to do it. As the CEO of Interstellar, it's my duty to go down swinging instead of being a passive bystander. I'll have my people on a solution night and day until it's resolved, leaving Interstellar intact, with me still sitting at the head.

I didn't work my ass off to become number two again, or worse, out of a job altogether.

When I decide they've waited long enough, I slowly walk to the lobby with my head held high and my shoulders back, ready to play hardball.

Show no fear.

They are the enemy.

My sleek black business suit caresses my skin, fitting me like a glove as I stroll down the hallway with my heels clicking against the marble floor. The sound of my power heels gives me a little more confidence and makes me feel powerful.

Every girl has a pair. The ones that make you feel fierce and unstoppable. Yesterday, I wasn't prepared; I didn't know about the Cozza shitstorm that was about to hit, or else I would've worn them. But now, I'm ready. Ready to cut the head off the snake that is trying to slither its way into my company and eat us alive.

Cassie walks toward me with a glass of water. "Sorry I didn't bring them sooner," she says, holding open her palm and revealing two white pills before shoving the glass between us.

I look over her shoulder as I take the aspirins from her palm, but I can't get a clear view of the reception area. "How are the Cozza people doing?"

She smiles, watching me swallow the pills before taking the glass back from me. "Annoyed."

I laugh.

Perfect.

"One guy is pacing around like a rabid animal." She giggles softly, covering her mouth to stop the sound from reaching their ears.

"Even better." I grin.

As I walk toward the reception area with Cassie on my heels, I feel a sense of calm wash over me. I know I can handle Cozza, and with the backing of the board and shareholders, there's no way they'll be a success in their takeover bid.

Four men are sitting, and the one that Cassie described as "rabid" still paces but his back is to me. "Gentlemen." I keep my face devoid of emotion.

Even though this feels personal, I know it isn't. They may have been trying to take Interstellar, but it isn't mine. Either way, I'll do anything I can to stop them.

The pacer stops, turning to face me as the other men stand.

Standing before me in a perfectly pressed black suit with dark gray pinstripes, a crisp white dress shirt, and a silky red tie is none other than the smooth-talking, panty-dropping charmer from last night.

Lou.

The Lou who was between my legs less than ten hours ago, giving me more orgasms than I've had in years.

I gape, unable to hide my shock.

What the hell? Nothing makes sense.

His face matches mine, confusion in his eyes as he takes in the sight of me. "Elizabeth?"

Chapter 6

His head tilts, his hair flopping a bit in the most delicious way, before he takes a step forward in impeccable black leather shoes.

I snap my mouth shut. "Lou?"

What's he doing here? Oh God. This can't be happening.

"Who?" Cassie whispers at my side. "That's Mr. Forte. His name isn't Lou. It's Antonio." She points at him, but it still hasn't clicked.

The people in the waiting room are gawking at us.

I blink twice, wondering if he is a mirage. There's no denying that the man standing in front of me is the same man I had sex with more than once last night. We stare at each other, both considering the ramifications of the situation.

Oh, shit.

I lied about my name, but I never imagined he could be the enemy. Why in the world would he lie about his name?

My palms begin to sweat, and my heart starts to pick up speed as the reality of the situation hits me. Maybe he played me. I was just another pawn in the Cozza game. I rarely believe anything is coincidence.

I take a step forward, my eyes narrowing at him. "Did you know?"

He shakes his head and gawks at me. "No."

A gentleman coughs and steps in front of Mr. Forte. "I don't know what's going on here, Ms. Bradley, but we're here to discuss the future of Cozza and Interstellar. I'm Mr. Alesci, the president of Cozza's legal division." He holds out his hand, but I don't meet his eyes as I shake. I'm unable to take mine off Antonio.

I'm still in a trance, maybe in shock, about the entire Lou situation. I shake Mr. Alesci's hand and keep my eyes pinned to Mr. Forte. "Excuse me," I say, glancing at Mr. Alesci for a moment before bringing my eyes back to the sky-blue ones boring into me. "Mr. Forte, may I speak to you in private please?"

"I don't think—" Mr. Alesci starts to say before Mr. Forte places his hand on his shoulder and gives it a rough squeeze.

"Yes, Ms. Bradley." Mr. Alesci glares at Antonio but is quickly dismissed. "We'll be fine, Jim."

Turning my back to him, I let every facial expression I wanted to make before break loose. What in the fuck just happened? How in the world could this be happening to me? What are the odds of the one person I sleep with in longer than I'd like to admit would actually be the one person I'm supposed to hate the most?

There's a real possibility that he played me. It's entirely possible that he knew exactly who I was when he sidled up next to me at the bar. Just because I didn't know who he was doesn't mean he didn't know who I was last night.

Antonio follows closely as we walk into my office. Using one hand, I close the door quietly, trying to avoid any more suspicion. "You knew who I was, didn't you?" My nostrils flare, and I know I'm the one who looks like a rabid animal now.

"I didn't." He takes a step toward me.

I hold up my hand, stopping him. If he comes any closer, I'll likely have a meltdown. "Stop."

"I swear I didn't know!"

The long night hasn't made him look any worse for wear. He looks more handsome than he did last night, while I, on the other hand, am not at my best. I cross my arms over my chest and stare him down. "How could you?"

"I didn't know. I swear. Why did you lie about your name?"

My teeth are clenched so tightly that they scrape against each other, making a horrible noise and making my headache worse. "Why did you lie about yours?"

He lets out a loud sigh and moves toward me, but I take a step back and bump into the door. He runs his fingers through his perfectly styled hair and inhales. "I don't need someone looking me up online and thinking they hit the jackpot. I never use my real name to anyone unless I know them well."

Unconsciously, my head tilts and my eyes narrow. "So, every woman you've slept with thinks you're Lou?"

"No." He rubs the back of his neck. "Some think I'm Fabio, Angelo, Salvatore, Giovanni—" he says with a small laugh.

"I get it," I interrupt him, totally disgusted.

"Why did you lie?"

"None of your business."

He squares his shoulders and pins me in place with his searing blue eyes. "I should be asking you if you knew who I was, Ms. Bradley."

"Do you honestly think I would've slept with you if I knew who you were?" I snarl, ready to pop from anger at the accusation.

"We didn't sleep," he corrects me with a salacious smile.

"Don't play games."

"I'd never play games when it comes to you or my business."

"Neither do I. To accuse me of having sex with you on purpose is sickening."

"You accused me of the same thing, Lauren." The sound of my real name on his tongue seems wrong, but completely delicious.

"Touché." Crossing my arms, I dig my fingernails into the skin of my arms. I want to stop myself from reaching out to touch the stubble on his face.

He's the enemy. No matter what happened last night, I need to remember that simple fact.

"What a mess," I whisper.

"It's a small complication." He waves it off like it isn't that important.

"You're right. It was just sex, and this is business."

He nods with a smile. "We're adults."

"Yes. What happened last night will never happen again." Even though I'm able to keep my voice steady, I know that if circumstances were different, I'd quickly jump back into bed with him.

He's just that good.

"No?" He raises an eyebrow as his smile transforms into the smuggest grin I've ever seen.

With a pin-straight spine and my head held high, I say, "No."

For the love of God, only I would get myself into a mess like this. I can already hear the gossip if this got out. People are quick to judge and condemn females in the business world. Hell, anywhere in life, women are tossed to the side and called whores. I don't want to ruin my reputation with an act between two consenting adults.

After I open the door, I wait for him to walk out. I don't want him behind me, checking out my ass. When he has one foot in the doorway, he stops and turns to face me.

"Lauren," he says, rolling the R on his tongue. "Business is always separate from pleasure. We may be in the middle of a business deal, but I need to spend another night with you. There's something about the way you moan that kind of drives me wild."

My insides are cheering, my belly is flipping, and every nerve ending in my body craves the feel of him against me again. "It'll never happen again."

He moves in closer, his lips a breath away from mine. "It will."

My breath hitches.

Damn.

The last man in the world I want to show weakness in front of is Antonio Forte, and yet I do it.

Bravo, Lauren.

His eyes dip to my mouth. "You know you want me too."

I remember the taste of him and shiver. "I don't," I whisper.

His eyes return to mine, his cheeks rising with a cocky smile. "You do," he says before walking out the door and heading toward the reception area, leaving me behind.

I want to scream and tell him he's wrong, but he isn't.

I do want him.

I'm so screwed.

I take a moment to collect myself before following him out. Nothing will go as planned, but I need to remember this is business, and like all business transactions, it will be cutthroat.

Kill or be killed.

I don't plan on being the victim ever again.

■ ■ ■ ■ ■ ■ ■ ■

Antonio hasn't taken his eyes off me since we sat down at the conference room table. Nothing else in the room seems to matter. Even the voices around me become muffled. He sits directly across from me with a smug grin on his face. Every so often his eyes dip to my chest, but they don't linger long enough for anyone to pick up on it. I want to leap across the table and smack the smile off his face.

"We came here today to talk about the future." Antonio's tongue darts out, sweeping across his bottom lip, and I try not to gawk. "As you know by now, we purchased a substantial stake in Interstellar and plan to snap up as much stock as we can get our hands on in the coming week."

I glare at him and lean forward. "Why now?" He doesn't have to answer the question because I already know the answer. Somehow Cozza found out about our newest invention, and they want it as their own.

"Why not now?" His head tilts, and his grin grows a little wider as he strokes the stubble on his chin. The same hair that felt like velvet gliding across my thighs.

I clench my legs together and take a deep breath before swallowing down my anger and lust. This is not personal. "You could've done this at any time, but you chose this week to start your takeover bid of Interstellar, why?"

Antonio rests his elbows on the table and clasps his hands together. "There have been rumors for some time about the advancements Interstellar is making, and you've caught the attention of Cozza and, of course, me." His eyes sparkle on the last word.

I clear my throat and try not to remember how he looked between my legs, but I fail, squeezing my legs together tighter. "Rumors?"

"Yes." He smiles, staring intently at me and causing my body temperature to rise.

Underneath the table, I uncross my legs, trying to take the edge off the ache his nearness causes. Why did he have to be good in bed? This would be so much easier if he were a bad lay. I wouldn't be imagining the feel of him as he filled me, the sound of his breath in my ear, or how he tasted in my mouth. "Every employee here has signed a nondisclosure agreement. So are you telling me I have a traitor in my midst?" I raise my eyebrows, challenging him to leak the name of their source.

"No traitor at all. People talk, Ms. Bradley. Companies watch the smaller ones, the ones underneath us." He licks his lips again, and I remain still, transfixed by the motion. "We're always looking to acquire those in need of help."

I square my shoulders and clasp my hands together much like his and blink away my Lou haze. "I don't know what you've heard, Mr. Forte, but Interstellar isn't in need of help. Is the competition getting a little too tough that you feel the need to take out your competition before they crush you?" It's my turn to smirk. Take that, Lou.

He glances down both sides of the table at his men and laughs. "I hardly call Interstellar competition, but I would like to take you over."

I swallow, wondering if he's talking about me or Interstellar. "We don't need your help. We don't want to be enveloped by Cozza and their worldwide conglomerate. We're doing just fine without your help, Antonio. Do you mind if I call you Antonio?"

He blinks slowly with a lazy grin. "You may call me anything you'd like, Ms. Bradley."

"Bastard," I whisper under my breath. "We appreciate your offer, but I've already discussed the takeover with the board members and majority stockholders, and no one is chomping at the bit to become one with Cozza."

He runs his index finger across his bottom lip. "There's no one better to become one with, Ms. Bradley. Cozza has ruled the industry for years, and it's better to be part of number one than to take second place."

"Mr. Forte," Josh interrupts and begins to tap his pen on the table. "Interstellar has no need for your offer and will fight you tooth and nail to stop the takeover in its tracks."

Antonio turns his attention toward Josh. The playful smile that had been on his face vanishes. "I believe I'm speaking to your CEO, Mr...?" Antonio's eyebrows furrow as he motions toward Josh.

"I'm the vice president," Josh bites out, clearly irritated by his dismissal.

"Ah. So, you're second-string in a second-place company."

Josh's body stiffens, and he starts to rise from his chair. "Excuse me?"

I grab his hand, stopping him from turning this into a free-for-all. "Mr. Forte, I don't appreciate how you're speaking to my VP. I understand you want to discuss the situation with me, but Mr. Goldman is a valuable member of the team, and I'd appreciate it if you treated him with the respect he deserves."

He nods, but he gives away no emotion. "Fine, Ms. Bradley. You can say that Interstellar doesn't want any part of Cozza, but we're here to make it known that we fully intend to take what we want, with or without your cooperation."

"Duly noted, Mr. Forte." I smile sweetly, almost over the top. "We decline your offer and plan to do everything in our power to crush your attempt to take over our little company. Just so you know, you can't stay on top forever."

He bites his lip to hide his smile, but the tiny crinkles in the corners of his beautiful eyes deepen. "I beg to differ. I can stay on top for a very long time. There's no limit to our domination, even over you, Ms. Bradley. I've never been one to play nice. Even with a woman across the table, I won't be a gentleman."

"Don't think my gender means I'm weak, Mr. Forte. I'm one of the toughest opponents you'll ever face. Interstellar will fight you every step of the way. Now, I have a corporation to run. I don't have time to sit here and discuss your pipe dreams. I'm too busy edging Cozza out of their top spot to worry about your attempts to take us over. We've survived other attempts just as we'll survive Cozza's."

His blue eyes bore into me. "Maybe we can come to a mutually beneficial agreement."

I glare at him, squeezing my legs together again under the table to stop the ache when I think about him last night. "We don't want anything you have to offer. We have you running scared. You know you're about to lose the top spot, to a woman CEO no less, and you're scared, Mr. Forte."

His hands sweep down his tie, smoothing it against his shirt. "I'm never scared. We've told you about our plans. You've been warned." He rises from the chair, resting his knuckles on the table, and leans forward. "We will take what we want, Ms. Bradley, without apology or remorse."

I want to wipe the cockiness off his face, but I give him a small smile instead. "We look forward to crushing your dreams, Mr. Forte." I stand and walk toward the conference room door. "Good day, gentlemen." I hold it open for them to leave with a smile on my face. "Gentlemen." I try to play nice even though I want to trip each one on his way out.

Naturally, Mr. Forte's the last to leave and stops right in front of me. "Lauren." The sound of my name coming from his lips sends goose bumps across my flesh. "We aren't over."

I glance down as he extends his hand to me. "Mr. Forte, we have nothing further to discuss."

"I didn't get where I am by giving up, Ms. Bradley." He smirks.

My eyes drop to his mouth and he catches me, but I quickly regain my senses. "My assistant will show you out."

"Why don't you walk with me?"

"I'll show him out," Josh says, barging in between us.

"I'd rather be shown out by Ms. Bradley, but thank you, Mr. Gold."

Josh's jaw ticks. "It's Goldman."

Antonio waves him off. "Ms. Bradley, please." He holds out his arm, waiting for me to walk in front of him.

Like the professional I am, I strut out of the room with Antonio close on my heels. I won't give him the satisfaction of showing me up in my own company. Even though I like to say it's only business, it's personal too. I've tasted the man, felt him deep inside me, and he knew exactly what I sounded and looked like when I came.

"See me again," he whispers in my ear when we are separated from the group.

I keep my face forward, ignoring him.

"Lauren, we need to talk about what happened." His voice sounds more urgent and needy.

"There's nothing to discuss, Lou." I smile at the group in front of us after one of them turns around.

"There's plenty to discuss. Business aside, Lizzy, we need to speak. Meet me for dinner," he pleads, picking up the pace to match my steps as I try to hurry the walk along and get him out of there.

"No," I snap and finally turn to look at him. "I want nothing from you."

"You do." He smirks.

I can't stop glaring at him. "I don't."

"Lauren, you know no one made you—" He brings his mouth closer to my ear. "Come as hard as I did."

My eyes widen. I pray no one overheard his statement. I scan the crowd, but no one seems to be paying us any attention. "Fuck off, Lou," I hiss, unable to hide my emotion any longer. "There's nothing between us and never will be."

"Just because you say the words doesn't make them true." He smiles like the Cheshire cat and moves far enough away from me that I can't reply without being overheard. "I'll exchange contact information with your assistant and be in touch."

Asshole.

"Gentlemen, thank you for coming today," I say to the group as they stand near the elevators. "I hope never to see you again." My words are aimed directly at Antonio. I smile and turn on my heel, marching toward my office with my head held high.

Screw Cozza and Antonio Forte.

They aren't going to win this battle.

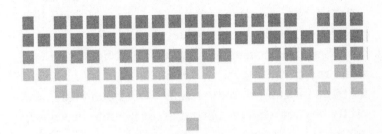

Chapter 7

My eyes scan the offices as I walk down the hallway. I take pride in knowing I helped build this company into something bigger, stronger than it had been before. The hundreds of employees moving around the building depend on me to bring Interstellar into the top position. Each one has devoted their life to the company and given their blood, sweat, and tears. I can't hand them over to Cozza and Forte to pink slip without so much as a second thought.

In some ways, working at Interstellar to advance the aerospace industry was for my father. I wanted him to be proud. I wanted to reach for the stars like he'd always dreamed. I'll be damned if I let a man— let alone a cock, come between me, my team, and the company.

Just as my bottom touches the chair, Josh marches into my office in a tizzy. "What the hell was that?" He tugs on his cuff links like he's trying to regain his composure.

"I don't know what you mean, Josh." I lean back, relaxing into the cool leather material, and kick off my shoes.

"There's something going on, Lauren. I don't like how Antonio talked to or looked at you."

"It's just business. He's a man and figures he can rattle me because I'm a woman. Little does he know that he's messing with the wrong CEO. I don't care how pretty he is or what comes out of his mouth—he's never getting this company."

"Who's pretty?" Trent asks, striding into my office like he owns the space.

I close my eyes, wishing them both away.

"She thinks Forte is pretty," Josh replies for me and laughs.

Trent glares at me. "You do?"

I clench my jaw so tightly that my teeth squeak. "I didn't say that."

Josh gives me a look that screams bullshit.

"Josh, are we done here?" I ask, fisting my hands in my lap under the desk so neither of them can see. "Where's the team on squashing the Cozza deal?"

Josh glances between us, giving Trent a once-over before leaving. "I'll check."

"What do you want, Trent?" I shuffle papers around on my desk, trying to organize the chaos that has taken place in the last twenty-four hours.

Trent sits down, smoothing out his tie as he leans back in the chair. "So, when do I get to test the engine, Lulu?"

My hands stop over one pile, and I can't believe something so huge has slipped my mind. In the frenzy yesterday, I forgot to call Trent and give him the go-ahead. "Damn," I hiss and slam the stack on top of another.

"What's wrong?"

I glare at him. "Just a lot on my mind. You can start the final test phase. The board was excited to hear about it, and your team received unanimous support." I fiddle with my necklace, running my fingers back and forth along the chain, and watch him. "We ran into a possible complication."

He moves forward, and he places his elbows on his knees, staring at me. "What happened?"

"Cozza."

He hangs his head briefly before bringing his eyes back to mine. "I heard some whispers, but I figured it was bullshit. What did they do now?"

"They're trying to take us over. I think they know about the engine and that we're in a final test phase. Any idea how they could know about it?" I keep my eyes on him. Not even risking a blink because I might miss something in his body language.

His eyes widen. "No!"

"Be honest with me."

He clasps his hands in front of his body and squeezes, his knuckles turning white from the grip. "Lauren, I swear. It wasn't me. You know I'm loyal to you."

I take a deep breath, searching him for a moment. "I know you are." I do. Trent wants me, but that doesn't mean he can't be bought. "But the question is, are you loyal to Interstellar?"

His hand flies to his chest as he gapes at me. "I can't believe you'd ask me that."

Classic deflection. I cross my arms in front of myself, trying to hold my anger in before I do something I'll regret. "You didn't answer the question."

"Of course, I'm loyal," he bites out through gritted teeth.

I chew the inside of my mouth. He may say the words, but it doesn't mean I believe the conviction in his voice. Though, it wouldn't make sense for him to sell out Interstellar. Trent has the highest position for a man in his field—it's his dream job. Plus, he has free rein to work on any project he wants because it's the only time I've never told him no.

"Okay, Trent. I have an important phone call I need to make."

He rises to his feet and hovers over my desk. "Want to get a drink after work?"

I purse my lips before transforming them into a smile. "Sorry, Trent. I'm too busy for drinks these days. There's a hostile takeover in place, and it's all hands on deck."

Trent hovers closer. "I'd like to have my hands on your—"

"Get out." I point toward the door and rise from my chair quickly. "Trent, really. Usually, I'm more patient with you, but not today."

He laughs softly, tipping his head back. "You were never patient, Lulu." He walks out without saying another word, and I feel like shit for treating him so harshly—for approximately twenty seconds until my phone chirps.

Unknown: Meet me for dinner.

"What's up, fearless leader?" Cassie asks, walking into my office and carrying a new pile of papers. "This desk is a mess."

"Ya think, Cas? You think you can help with it? I've lost track at this point."

She nods and starts going through each folder and forming new piles on the chairs in my office. I take the time to check my email. My phone chirps again, but I ignore it.

Cassie's gaze drifts toward my phone. "Oh, you have an admirer." She giggles and waggles her eyebrows.

I snatch the phone from my desk and turn it over to hide the screen. "It's the wrong number, Cassie. Shush it." I wink at her.

"Um," she says, rolling her eyes. "Yeah. You're right. They're looking for Elizabeth."

My stomach plummets. The air from my lungs evaporates into thin air at the thought of Antonio being the "Unknown" texter. "Yeah, wrong number." I slide the button on my phone to silence any other notification. I can't look until she leaves the room.

"I wish a man would send me random steamy text messages."

"It was steamy?"

She whistles. "Whoever Lizzy is—" She stops mid-sentence and turns to look at me. Her eyes are wide as she blinks rapidly. "Wait! Mr. Forte called you Lizzy.

Damn." She points at my phone, looking between it and me.

I shake my head and try to keep my face unexpressive. "Don't be silly. You must've heard him wrong." I glance down at my computer screen, unable to look her in the eyes and lie. "He thought I was someone he knew from college, but he was wrong."

"Umm." She sweeps her finger along the edge of my desk as she takes steps around the back. "I know I can seem like I'm an airhead sometimes, Lauren, but I heard him clear as day, and he didn't think you were someone else."

"Cassie," I warn, keeping my eyes on the screen. "Drop it."

She stands by my side, tapping her fingernails on top of the giant pile of to-do papers. "As you know, as your employee, I signed a nondisclosure agreement. Whatever I know, I can't divulge."

With someone selling us out to Cozza, I don't put much stock in a nondisclosure or any promise to keep anything in confidence. Cassie and I have always been more than employer and employee. She's been with me since the beginning and has always been the one I lean on in times of need. Her ability to listen and give good advice is priceless to me. Even though sometimes she doesn't clean my desk, she is worth her weight in gold.

"I'm not firing you, but from now on, ask before you give out my personal cell phone number. I swear, Cas. There's nothing going on between him and me."

"Look me in the eyes and say it." She smirks.

I cross my fingers under my desk and peer up at her. "I swear there's nothing."

She nods and looks disappointed. "Too bad. He was kind of hot." She fans herself with her hand.

I grimace because she isn't lying–he's hot as hell. "If that's the type of guy you like."

"You can say whatever you want, but I saw the way you looked at him."

"You mistake lust for hate. I don't want to sleep with him, I want to pound him into pieces."

"Pound," she whispers through her giggles.

"Don't you have work to do?" I ask, feeling uncomfortable having this conversation about Antonio, especially when everything I say sounds filthy.

"I do. I'd better go pound the keys like I'd pound..."

"Out," I tell her and shoo her away with a giant smile. "I'll finish organizing my paperwork."

"I'm sorry. I'll behave, Ms. Bradley."

I can't help but laugh. "I've never known you to behave when it comes to men, Cas."

"There's a time to work, and then there's a time to play." She grabs a stack from the couch in the back of the room and heads for the door. "I'm going to go work before I get myself in some trouble."

"Thanks." I walk toward the two chairs in front of my desk to see what papers were in the stack and hope I can figure out her process.

"Call me if you need me." She closes the door and leaves.

As soon as I hear her footsteps far enough away from my office, I bolt toward my desk and grab my phone.

Unknown: I need to taste you again, Elizabeth.

Unknown: I want more than your company.

Unknown: Same time, same place–tonight.

Clearly, the man is crazy if he thinks I'll meet him again. Last night was one of the biggest mistakes of my life...and the hottest one too. But knowing who he is, I can't do it. Even if it was the best sex of my life, we are at war.

I try to work and get my head on straight, but my eyes keep peering down at my phone, waiting for the next message. "I'm an idiot." I push my body back into my chair and close my eyes. When my phone chirps again, I can't stop myself from looking.

Unknown: Lou will be waiting for Liz.

Fuck, what a mess.

"Lauren," Josh says, giving the door a quick knock out of respect, but he's already two strides inside my office. "Do you have time for a meeting? Our team has some ideas on how to stop the takeover by Cozza."

I jump up from my seat because having news about a way to halt them in their tracks is just what I need. "I always have time when it comes to Interstellar."

"Walk with me." He moves to the side, having me walk in front of him, but he's following close on my heels. "Our options are limited, but it's entirely possible to stop their bid."

"I've always liked a challenge, Josh. No matter what it is, we'll make it work." I push open the door to the conference room to find the entire legal division assembled around the table. "Good afternoon, everyone."

"Good afternoon, ma'am." Mr. Wiggins, the head of the legal team, greets me by standing.

"Sit, sit." I motion for them to remain seated as I start to pace. "What have you been able to find?"

Wiggins clears his throat and glances down at his paperwork. "There are a few things we have going for us that can stop Cozza in their tracks." He holds up a handful of paperwork and looks in my direction. "First, your contract should be reason enough to have them running for the hills."

I freeze and turn on my heel to face him. "How so?"

"Built into your contract, as with every CEO before you, there's a clause designed to stop such maneuvers. You were given an enormous golden parachute payoff that no company will want to swallow in order to take over Interstellar."

I gulp down the lump that's suddenly formed in my throat. "How much?" I ask, clenching my jaw when I try to control my breathing.

"Twenty million." He smiles like he's a genius and a savior, but his find is not a saving grace.

The golden parachute clause in my contract had totally slipped my mind. I never gave it another thought after I signed the paperwork the day I became CEO. Now it adds an entirely new dimension of shit that could fall at my feet by sleeping with Antonio. Not only would I profit substantially from being removed as CEO and the purchase of Interstellar, but people could say I did it on purpose. I knew how rumors worked. Not only could he ruin my company, he could destroy my reputation. I know the clause was added to stop someone from buying us, but with the new engine we are on the verge of releasing, our acquisition would still be a financial gain for any potential purchaser.

Unconsciously, I start to pace again, worry filling my entire body. "It's not good enough, Wiggins. We need to find another way to stop them."

His eyebrows furrow. "You don't feel the parachute will be sufficient?"

I shake my head, blowing out a puff of air. "It's not when you think of the financial gain that our new engine could bring to the purchaser. It's not enough, Mr. Wiggins." My palms are sweaty, and I suddenly feel flushed.

"Well, we do have another way." He pauses and relaxes back in his chair, watching me like a hawk.

I grip the back of the chair tightly. "Out with it," I bark out, unable to control the fear that has consumed me.

"We need to make sure we have a supermajority of stockholders that do not want to sell to Cozza. Cozza has to have the backing of that majority in order to gain control of Interstellar and be successful in their hostile takeover."

"How many?" I ask, tapping my finger against the back of my chair.

"Over seventy percent of stockholders must agree not to sell their shares, Ms. Bradley." Wiggins straightens his shoulders but never takes his eyes off me.

"We can do that." I glance toward the ceiling and start to pace again, forming a plan in my head. "We need to call an emergency stockholder meeting to unveil the technology and announce the date of the public test. For the people who can't be there, we'll do a simultaneous webcast for our shareholders around the world where we'll unveil our newest invention that's going to catapult Interstellar to the top spot."

"That may take some time," Josh interrupts. "Also, I feel we should maybe test the engine privately first."

I stop behind his chair. "Although it may seem like the most sensible option, under the circumstances, it's vital that we make it public to shore up our stock. So, make it happen. You have thirty-six hours, Josh. Give me a goddamn miracle."

Although I can't see his face, his posture tells me everything I need to know. Josh is tense, but not a traitor. Everything about his demeanor confirmed that before we walked into the meeting. "I can work with thirty-six hours, Ms. Bradley," Josh replies and starts to tap his pen against the papers in front of him.

"In the meantime, we need to draft a letter to all shareholders of the company. They need to be made aware of the takeover attempt by Cozza. Tell them we have something on the horizon that will make them filthy rich, and if they sell now, they'll regret it. Invite them to the meeting where we'll unveil the engine and show them that selling now will be the costliest decision of their lives."

"Between a supermajority and your golden parachute, I can't see Cozza moving forward with the acquisition of Interstellar, Ms. Bradley," Wiggins adds while the rest of the legal team remains quiet.

"Good. Anyone have anything else before we adjourn?"

"No, ma'am. We'll get everything in order legally speaking to deal with unveiling the invention early and solidifying our position from Cozza."

I give him a brief nod and wait for them to file out one by one before turning toward Josh. "We have a mole, Josh."

"I know. I've been racking my brain trying to figure out who it could be." He drags his hands through his dark hair and groans. "Who would want to bring down Interstellar when we're so close to greatness?" His hand comes down hard on the table, causing the pitcher of water sitting in the center to bounce.

"I don't know, Josh, but I'm going to find out."

I lie down on the couch, draping my arm over my face to give my eyes a rest. I've been staring at the computer for hours, and my vision has started to blur. "Cassie, you can go now. It's late, and there's nothing more you need to do tonight."

"Can I get you anything before I go?" She yawns on the last word.

"No. I can get whatever I need. Go home, Cas. I kept you here far too late."

"I wanted to stay and help, but thank you, Lauren."

Although I am exhausted, I feel we have a grasp on the situation. The rest of the day I'd spent drafting my speech to the stockholders, to expand on the letter written by our PR department, to help get them excited about the engine and greedy for the money that will flow into their pockets when Interstellar overtakes Cozza as the industry leader in the aerospace market. I yawn, letting myself succumb to the exhaustion.

Soft, warm lips touch mine, and I moan softly. Rarely do I have dreams that involve sex in any form. It's a nice change. The softness grows more demanding, pressing harder against my mouth. I gasp, realizing it isn't a dream at all. Someone's in my office and has their lips pressed against mine.

I push against his chest with one hand, but I can't move. His body is against me, rock solid and strong. "Get away from me!" I yell against his mouth.

"Lulu, come on. It's just me," he murmurs against my lips.

"Trent, stop!" I wiggle underneath him, trying to break free. I have one card to play, and I use it. Biting down hard, I dig my teeth into his lip and break the skin.

He screeches and recoils, giving me the ability to move finally. His hand covers his mouth, and his eyes flare with anger. "What the fuck, Lulu?" he seethes, wiping the blood away and smearing it across his cheek. He glances down, catching sight of his blood. "Fucking bitch."

I shoot up from the couch, squaring my shoulders and placing my arms in front of me. "I should fire your ass for this. You can't just come in here and kiss me. I'm not yours anymore, Trent."

He comes toward me with a devilish smile stained red from the blood. "Why do you lie to yourself? You'll always be mine."

"I won't." I point toward the door, readying my leg in case I need to knee him in the balls. "Get the fuck out before I call security."

"Baby," he whispers, reaching out to touch me. "You know how I know you're still mine?" He stops a foot from me and sucks his lip inside his mouth.

I don't respond. My entire body shakes with anger and partially out of fear, but I'd never let him know that. I'm not worried that his words are true, but I never would've guessed Trent could be so aggressive toward me.

"You moaned like a whore when I kissed you—my whore, Lulu. No matter what you say, you can never be without me."

My teeth are clenched so tightly they vibrate from the friction. "Fuck you, Trent. I may value your work, but there is not now and never will be anything between us. Next time you come into my office uninvited, bring your letter of resignation with you."

He throws his hands up in the air and laughs. "I was just kidding. I'm just having a little harmless fun. When did you get so damned uptight?"

"There was nothing harmless about you pinning me to the couch and putting your filthy hands on me."

His laughter stops, but the smile remains. "You forgot about my lips."

I stomp to the door and fling it open. "Get out!"

He doesn't move, just stands there with a smile. "I came here to talk to you about the engine."

"I don't care what you came here for, I'm done."

He walks toward me, stopping in front of me, but he keeps his hands to himself. "But, Lulu, come on. It's important."

"We'll talk tomorrow, Trent. Get out before I change my mind and fire you."

He runs his tongue across his lips, but I don't dare glance down. In no way would I ever give him any indication that I could be even remotely attracted to him. "You would never do that, babe."

"Try me," I say, crossing my arms over my chest and glaring at him. "Three." I start a countdown. If I get to zero and his ass isn't out of my office, I'll officially and happily fire him. "Two."

"Fine," he growls. "I'll be here first thing in the morning."

"Fine!" My temper's boiling over. "Cassie and Josh will be joining us."

"Doesn't matter to me. No one can stop me from having you again, Lulu." He reaches out and brushes his fingers against my cheek.

I jolt back, moving away from his touch, and swat his hand. "One."

"I'm out." He leaves quickly, tucking his hands into his pockets as he heads toward the elevators.

I stand in my doorway, making sure he's left before gathering my things and heading down the stairwell and out of the building. Between Cozza and Trent, I'm close to a breakdown. Everything I've worked for sits precariously on the edge of destruction.

With one flight of stairs left, my eyes start to flood with tears, and my knees begin to shake. The enormity of the situation, coupled with Trent, finally hits me like a ton of bricks. I collapse, crumpling down, and cry into my hands.

How could I be so stupid to get into a relationship with someone like Trent? I've never seen him act the way he has toward me, and it scares me. Although sometimes he can be overbearing and a little too touchy for me, never has he been so aggressive.

Everything in my life's a freaking train wreck.

I messed up by sleeping with Antonio, even though I didn't know it was him. It was reckless and could bring me down faster and harder than I'd ever imagined.

I'm on a collision course that only I could halt. I wipe away my tears and smooth out my suit as I stand. I don't have time for crying. It will solve nothing. Business people don't cry. I'm too powerful to let any man think I'm their plaything or underestimate me because I'm a woman.

I've come too far to take it all lying down. My father told me that I should rely only on myself. That I was too smart and driven to let anything derail my plans. He taught me to be who I am today. When he died, I didn't forget a word he said. In fact, I've tried to remember every word he'd ever spoken to me. I want him to be proud of me for my accomplishments, but also for the person I'd become. I am him. Part of him lives on in me, and I'll do anything to make him proud. Sometimes, when I'm lonely, I stare up at the stars and wonder if he's up there, watching me from afar. Even if there isn't a heaven, maybe there is a way he lived his dreams even after his light went out.

■ ■ ■ ■ ■ ■ ■ ■

I stroll into the W Hotel just past eight p.m. Antonio sits in the same seat as before, waiting for me with a martini ready. The first part of my plan is to find out if he set me up. It's hard to believe that I wasn't targeted for complete and total destruction.

Sleeping with me would be a surefire way to seal the deal and be the last straw. He toys with the glass in his hand and checks his watch before he takes a sip. Standing in the back, I stare at him for a few minutes, trying to work up the courage to approach him. Coming to a stop behind him, I clear my throat and wait for him to turn around.

"Ah, Elizabeth," he says, turning his head with a smile and setting his glass down on the bar. "I'm glad you could come."

"Antonio." I'm not going to play the game and use the fake name he gave me. There is no time for it. "I won't be staying."

"Lauren, please." He pats the stool next to him and motions for me to sit. "Have a drink with me. Not as enemies, but as..."

My back straightens, and I plant my feet shoulder width apart. "Mr. Forte, I'm sorry to burst the illusion, but we'll always be enemies."

"Nonsense." He waves me off, pushing the drink closer to the edge. "I got your favorite." His blue eyes twinkle from the halogen lighting overhead.

"I'm sure you're not always a bastard, but no drink will make up for what you're doing to me."

He laughs, tipping his head back and showing off his perfectly white teeth framed by his lusciously full lips. "Lauren, I'm not doing anything to you."

I set my purse on the bar and slide across the stool, but I keep my body as far away from him as possible. "You're trying to steal my company and ruin me in the process."

He touches his lip, slowly pulling his finger back and forth. "I'm not trying to ruin you. What would give you that crazy idea?"

I glare at him, not willing to back down from my statement as I raise the glass to my lips. Taking a small sip, I formulate my next statement very carefully before speaking. "You sought me out on purpose, Antonio. You knew exactly what you were doing when you seduced me right in this very spot. I may be a woman, but I'm not stupid."

His body jerks backward. "I would never," he scoffs and shakes his head vigorously.

"You did," I sneer before taking another sip.

"I had no idea who you were when I sat down next to you. I was lonely and looking for a little company." He grabs his drink, whiskey, from the looks of it, and turns it in his hand. "I didn't seek you out to fuck you."

"But you did fuck me."

"I did." His lips turn up into a smile, and his eyes flash.

I cross my legs, trying to put all thoughts of sleeping with him out of my mind. "You did it on purpose. You're trying to ruin all credibility I have in this industry."

He raises his left eyebrow, forming a beautiful, dark arch. "How could sleeping with me ruin you?"

I gnaw on my lip. "It just can." I won't dare answer his question. I don't know why, but I don't feel the need to explain my accusation. "Why do you want Interstellar so badly?"

"You're poised to jump in front of Cozza. I'm used to being on top, Lauren, and nothing will keep me from staying there. Not you. Not Interstellar. Nothing."

"So, your plan is to take us over and halt any progress we've made in developing new technology." I watch him over the rim of my glass, avoiding staring at his mouth as he speaks.

"Don't play coy with me. I know what's going on at Interstellar." His finger traces the rim of the glass, slowly moving in a circle over the smooth edge. "You're beyond development and are ready to start the final test phase."

I laugh. "You know nothing."

"Believe what you'd like, but I know." He smiles smugly, but he gives nothing more away. Running my hand down my throat, I let my fingers linger near my cleavage. His eyes dip, following the line. "I plan to make it mine."

"I will fight to keep Interstellar. I'll never willingly hand over the reins to you, Lou." I grin, watching his eyes as they continue to follow my fingers while I stroke my skin.

He licks his lips, lazily dragging his tongue across before looking into my eyes. "I've never had a problem taking what I want, Ms. Bradley. Whether it's Interstellar or you, I like a good challenge."

I slide my finger to my neck. "I'm not for sale, Mr. Forte, and neither is Interstellar. Did you set this up? Did you have me followed before you showed up at the bar and seduced me?"

"Lauren, you give me too much credit. It was serendipity."

"I'll never fully believe I wasn't set up, and even if I wasn't and it was by chance, the answer is and always will be no."

He inches closer, his stool scraping against the floor. "I'm not a man who takes no for an answer." He moves his mouth close to my ear and speaks in a low, husky tone. "I remember how you taste, the way you moaned when you came, and how your body feels wrapped around me. You can deny it all you want, but I know you want more."

I choke on the martini. I tap my chest and try to clear the alcohol lingering in my throat. "I most certainly do not." My voice comes out strangled and the words unbelievable. Somehow, I thought it was a good idea to take a sip and pretend not to be bothered by his proximity and words, but it was an epic fail.

His hand snakes around my stool, resting on a high-back barstool and lightly brushing my back. "So, if I touched you right now, it wouldn't mean anything?"

My eyes shoot to his, the hatred in my glare unmistakable. "It would mean absolutely nothing."

One side of his mouth curves up before he moves forward, stopping centimeters from my lips. "May I?" he asks, staring me straight in the eyes when his hand touches my face, sliding behind my neck.

My body grows rigid, and I try to ready myself for his lips. The way he kissed me the other night was indescribable. The most passionate and intoxicating kisses of my entire life, followed by the hottest, rawest sex I've ever experienced. I know before his lips touch mine again that if I'm not careful, he'd know he was right. I wanted him, even though I hated him. The phrase there's a thin line between love and hate fit us perfectly. "Yes," I reply, my voice unwavering.

I hold my breath and close my eyes as he leans forward. It starts slow, his lips testing mine and his warm breath cascading across my face. My mind's fuzzy and drunk as the kiss grows more demanding. His tongue sweeps across my bottom lip, tasting me, and I open for him, sucking in a breath and making his air my own.

He moans, digging his fingers into the back of my neck and pulling my body closer to him. My one hand clutches the bar, holding on for dear life as he consumes my every thought and fantasy. I can't stop my body from moving toward him and into the kiss. I want him. I want to feel him inside me again, and no matter how hard I try to deny it, I can't stop the ache.

I push against his chest, trying to break the contact. Needing for it to end before it goes too far and I won't be able to recover. "Stop," I whisper into his mouth. He grunts and kisses me deeper. "Antonio, please."

Our lips stick together when he backs away. His fingers still dig into the back of my neck as his eyes search mine. "Please, what?" The softness of his thumb strokes my cheek, touching the corner of my mouth.

Chills rake my body from his touch alone, and I'm almost breathless from the aftereffects of his kiss. "We can't." No longer can I deny I want him, but that doesn't make it right.

"Why?" He doesn't blink or look away, just stares at me, waiting for a response.

I close my eyes, trying to steady my pulse that has been racing out of control since his lips touched mine. "It's not right. I can't risk my entire life for a fling."

"You think I just want to fuck you again for thrills?"

I break free from his grip and out of the trance his lips had put me in. "I don't care what you call it. It can never happen again."

"Lauren." He reaches out, stopping me by grabbing my wrist. "My goal for coming to Chicago was taking over Interstellar, but now..." He takes a deep breath, dragging his eyes up my body and finally meeting my glare.

I grab my purse off the bar and stand quickly. "You can't stop what you've started. We're at war, Mr. Forte. No matter how well you kiss, I'll never forget the simple fact that you're trying to destroy my company and, by default, me. We are nothing. We will never be more than enemies. Good evening, Antonio." I march off, my heels clicking against the black tile of the hotel bar as I make my way to the lobby. My knees shake with every step. The effect he has on me is undeniable, but under no circumstances can I allow anything to come between Interstellar and me, especially Antonio.

When I step outside, I press my body against the building and let it be my support while I catch my breath. How could I let this happen? I slept with the one man in the world who could end everything I've done professionally in my entire life. He's the one person who could destroy my reputation and ruin everything I've worked so hard to accomplish. If I'm not careful and allow myself another night of pleasure, it will be the proverbial nail in my coffin.

After smoothing out my suit, I tuck my purse under my arm and walk home.

Antonio Forte will not be my undoing.

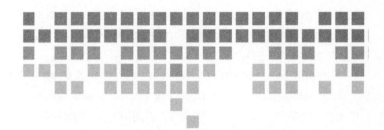

Chapter 8

I dreaded coming into work. The first thing on my agenda is meeting with Trent. After what happened last night, I don't want to see his face. I'd fire him if he weren't so valuable. But make no mistake about it, once the engine is out in the world, I'll have no problem giving him the ax.

"I'm here," Cassie exclaims when she crashes through the doors of my office with a coffee in her hand and a stack of folders tucked underneath her arm. "Sorry if I'm late."

"You're fine." I glance down at my watch before I continue typing out the rest of my email. "Trent will be here in five minutes."

She sets her coffee on the corner of my desk before placing the files on a side table near the back wall. "Why do you want me here for this meeting? You normally don't need a third person when meeting with Trent, Lauren."

I stop typing and give her my full attention. "I can't go into it, but it's best if I'm not alone with him anymore. Okay?" She nods and doesn't ask anymore.

Moments later and earlier than scheduled, Trent strides in without a care in the world. His chest's stuck out, hair perfectly placed, and a big shit-eating grin on his face. He glances to the side and jumps. "Oh. Cassie, I wasn't expecting you here."

She sits down in one of the empty chairs in front of my desk. "Ms. Bradley wanted me here to take notes." Her eyes flicker to mine with a small smile on her face.

"Please sit, Trent. Tell me what was so important that you had to barge into my office last night."

Cassie's eyebrows draw together, but I ignore her. She knows what happened between Trent and me when we broke up. She is an extension of me and knows everything that has gone on in my life.

"I thought..." He clears his throat and takes the seat next to Cassie, looking uncomfortable by her company. "I thought we could schedule the test flight with the new engine two days from now and invite the media."

I rub my chin and debate his suggestion. The media attention would boost our stock prices tremendously, but that could bite us in the ass. If the stock rises quickly to an unprecedented level, stockholders may be looking to sell and cash out, or they could see the potential wealth if they were patient enough to wait. If the test fails, it could cause our stock to drop dramatically and make Interstellar a bargain. "I'll talk to the PR department and get their input. If they allow it, we'll ask a few influential reporters to attend the final test before we unleash the engine and put it into our fleet."

"Yes!" His fists pump the air, and he has an enormous smile on his face. "I just want everyone to know about my creation."

"Our creation," I remind him. Even though he perfected it, I had helped. I came across an idea that was being tested in secret during World War II and thought the idea was feasible, even though they didn't have the technological ability to do it in the past. Interstellar had the means and money, and Trent had the brains and drive to pull it off.

His eyes shift. "Of course."

I clasp my hands together and rest them on the desk, trying to remain calm. "Is that all, Trent?"

He glares at me, his eyes narrowing before he glances in Cassie's direction. "I think that's it. I just want to make a splash."

"Just make sure it works flawlessly. If it doesn't, we're ruined, and your career will be as over as mine, Trent."

He pushes himself up and rests his knuckles against my desk. "Can I speak to you in private for a moment?"

"No. You can show yourself out." I peer around him and motion toward the door with my chin. "I'll email you when I have the details back from Trish in PR."

Leaning farther into my personal space, he speaks quietly. "Lulu, we have to talk about what happened."

There's nothing to discuss. Trent stepped over the line, basically attacking me in my office. If he'd done that to anyone else, I would've fired him immediately. Hell,

I should fire him anyway, but I can't bring myself to do it just yet.

I've never had a man so unwilling to let me go. I feel nothing for him except contempt, and no matter what I say, he can't seem to understand there will never be an us again.

"Trent," I say, pushing my chair back and rising to my feet just to get away from him and to stand my ground. "You have five seconds to get out of my office before I do something we'll both regret much like you did last night. Get out of my office, and don't come back unless I invite you back."

"Fuck," he hisses. There's a slight snarl on his lips when his nostrils begin to flare. "We're not done."

"Yes." I smile sweetly, tilting my head and squaring my shoulders. "We are."

"Goddamn it, Lulu." His arms flail a bit, and he lifts his hands from my desk and makes tight fists at his sides. "Just let me explain."

"Three."

"Shit," he groans, turning on his heel and heading toward the door too slowly.

"Two." I glance at Cassie, and her eyes are as big as saucers with her lips pursed.

"I'm gone," he calls out over his shoulder as he steps into the hallway.

Cassie stares at me, waiting for me to explain as I watch him walk away. "You don't want to know," I tell her, collapsing into my chair and pulling myself back in front of my desk. "He's lucky to have a job." Moving the mouse on my desk, I turn the screen back on to check my email to avoid having to answer any more questions about him.

"Do you need anything else, Lauren?"

I sigh, feeling a little bit of the weight that had been on my shoulders vanish. Kicking Trent out and standing my ground felt good. Better than that. It felt amazing, and I relished the look of defeat in his eyes. Maybe he finally realized we were over. There's no way in hell that anything will happen after the events of last night. "No, Cas, but if Trent ever needs to meet with me, I'll require you to be in the office with us."

Her eyes move around the room, and I can almost see the crazy, random thoughts in her eyes. "Yes, ma'am. You got it." She stands, clutching the pad of paper to her chest. "I'll contact PR about the test and get their feedback and have them contact you as soon as possible."

"Thanks." I genuinely smile at her because my heart has started to beat normally instead of the rapid pace from Trent being in the room.

"Anytime. Would you like some coffee?" she asks, moving toward the door.

"Vodka would be better." I laugh and wave her off.

When she walks out and closes the door, I put my head on my desk. A week ago, everything seemed possible, and I thought I had the world by the balls. How quickly shit can change. Life went from fab to crap in a hot minute, and I had no one to blame except myself.

"Ms. Bradley," Cassie says through the intercom, pulling me out of my thoughts.

"Yes?" I ask, my voice muffled by the wood of my desk.

"Tara is on the phone for you."

"Thank you." I shoot straight up and reach for the phone.

Tara is my best friend, been that way since we were little kids catching fireflies in the backyard. She's been through thick and thin, good and bad, and every point in between with me. I have to share the chaos that had become my life with someone, and she is just the person I need. She is far enough removed from Interstellar that I can be completely honest with her. She'd never betray my trust. I have too much dirt on her for her to ever open her mouth.

"Oh my God, T," I say after I press line one. "I need you."

"I've been calling for days, and you've ignored me. You do know how to pick up a phone and dial out without your secretary doing it for you, don't you?"

I grimace. She'd called me three times, and I hadn't picked up the phone to tell her I was still alive after she left me a profanity-laced voice mail days ago. "I'm sorry. Will you forgive me?"

"Don't I always?" she groans.

I laugh. "And Cassie is my assistant, not my secretary."

"She answers your phones-."

"Meet me for dinner tonight," I say quickly, interrupting her before checking my computer calendar. I'll cancel plans if I have them because tonight I need some girl time.

"Are you sure you have time for me? I mean, I know you're busy up there on your high horse."

"Shut up. Dino's at seven, or we're over."

"Dino's. Yum. Are you paying?" I owe her for canceling on her weeks ago, plus Dino's is pricey and I know she can't afford it on her artist income.

"Don't I always?"

"When you show up," she teases. "You'd better be there this time, or I'm ordering the most expensive bottle of wine on the menu and sending you the bill."

"I will be there. I need to talk with you. There's so much craziness going on right now. I can't get into it over the phone, but I need you to help me figure shit out."

"Sounds like a vodka kind of night."

"By the bottle, not glass. See you at seven. I have to run," I tell her, realizing I have a meeting in ten minutes.

"Later."

"Bye." I can't wipe the smile off my face as I hang up the phone. No matter what happens today, I know I will have Tara by my side tonight. Nothing makes me happier than my best friend and a bottle of vodka.

Some people go to church to confess their sins, but Tara is the only person who knows every part of my life. Tonight, I'll come clean, and with her help, figure a way out of the mess my life has turned into. With any luck, I'll escape without a hangover.

■ ■ ■ ■ ■ ■ ■

I walk into Dino's five minutes late, frantically power-walking through the door and colliding with a very tall man in a business suit. Trying to catch myself before my ass meets the floor, I reach out and grab the back of his arm. "Shit," I mutter, falling backward until strong arms grab me around the waist and steady me.

"Be careful there, Ms. Bradley."

My eyes widen at the sound of the voice. There's no way he could be at the same restaurant as me. No way in hell.

"Thanks," I say after regaining my footing, and I turn to stare into his beautiful eyes. "Antonio."

"Crazy running into you here." His eyes roam my body in the most sinful way. "Can I buy you a drink?" He grins.

"Are you following me?" I ask, peering up at him without a smile.

"No. I asked the concierge for a great Italian restaurant, and he recommended this place. It's pure coincidence. So, that drink?" He motions toward the bar.

I shake my head before peering over my shoulder and spotting Tara with a martini waiting for me at her side. "I'm meeting a friend." I turn back around to face him. "Sorry. I only drink with friends."

Being this close to him, no matter how much I want to hate him, I can't. I won't let my body betray me, though. I swallow down my nerves and ignore my heart beating against my ribs like it's ready to explode at any moment. "Another time maybe. Like when you lose and rot in hell." I smile, and before he can say another word, I walk away and head straight toward Tara.

"Who's that sexy as hell guy?" She watches Antonio from across the bar without even glancing in my direction.

"No one." I wave him off, but I don't look back. I can't.

"He's watching you," she says with the biggest smile on her face. "Oh, now he's waving."

"Fucker," I whisper. "Ignore him."

"Why?" She finally looks at me. "The man is sexy as fuck."

"He's no good, T. No good at all."

Her smile spreads across her face when she glances back in his direction. "He's waving at me." She waves back.

I grab her hand, pulling it down quickly and glaring at her. "Do not invite him over."

"Dude, you have a lot of explaining to do."

"Let's go. I can't eat here with him."

"Who said we're eating? I remember something about a bottle of vodka," she replies, pushing my martini in front of me.

"Can we just go? I'll take you anywhere you want to go."

"Fuck no. We're staying right here." She smiles, biting the corner of her lip. "Sit your ass down and drink with me. You have some things to tell me." She pats the stool next to her.

Before I can sit, Antonio makes his way to the bar and sits directly across from us with only the bartender's area between us. I close my eyes and try to calm myself before I blow a gasket. What was supposed to be a night to unwind has quickly become a mess.

I toss my purse on the bar. "I need this vodka." I grab the drink and down half of it before coming up for air. Tara gawks at me. "What?" I ask when I place the glass back on the bar.

"I haven't seen you this unraveled since..." Her voice trails off.

"Don't say it," I warn her as I sit down and try to act casual.

"Did you fuck him?" Her mouth drops open, and her eyes dart between Antonio and me.

Resting my elbow on the bar, I hold my head in my hand. "It's so much worse than that."

"You didn't let him do that, girl. I know you, and you don't get down like that."

I laugh softly. "Tara, be serious here for a minute."

"I am. I mean, I know I like to get freaky like that, but you usually don't unless you're really into the guy. If you gave him—"

"Stop," I groan, cutting her off from finishing the sentence.

"You better start talking, or I'm going to invite Mr. Tall, Dark, and Handsome over for a little drink and fun."

I lift the glass to my lips and stare at her as I let the cool, salty liquid slide down my throat. Even though I love her to death, I want to choke the funny right out of her. Her cute curly brown hair bounces as she fidgets on the stool. Her hazel eyes twinkle in the bar light every time she glances over at Antonio.

"Okay." I place the now empty martini glass down on the bar. "I don't even know where to start."

She rubs her hands together and smiles. "I want every juicy detail." She shrugs off her cardigan. "Wait, let me get comfier. I have a feeling your story is going to make me a little hot." She laughs and places the sweater across her lap.

I roll my eyes and motion to the bartender for a refill. "So, there's a company trying to take over Interstellar."

"Lauren, seriously. I want to know about him." She points at him and winks.

I cover my eyes, leaning against the bar for support. "Put your fucking hand down."

"I want the dirt, or I'll ask him." She motions with her head this time. "I'm sure he'll be more than willing to spill the dirt."

"Bitch."

"Yep. Talk."

"Shut up for a minute, and let me tell you the story." She nods and makes a motion like she's zipping her lips shut, and I inhale before diving into my speech. "Well, there's a company trying to take us over. I was so upset that I ended up at the bar and had a little too much to drink, and well..." I wince at the memory. "I ended up in his hotel room for the night."

"Oh my God! Was it amazing?"

"Tara, it's his company trying to take Interstellar from me."

"Let's plot his death." She stares at him as she takes a drink of her martini.

I stare at her, completely in shock. "Be serious."

"I am," she mutters against the rim of her glass. "If someone is trying to hurt you, I'd cut off his balls and shove them down his throat."

"Cool your jets, Scarface. I have this handled," I lie and try not to grind my teeth in aggravation.

Her face drops, and she looks over at me with sadness in her eyes. "That's such a shame. I thought we could have some fun."

"Tara." I grab her arm. "He's trying to steal my company, but not my life."

"Same thing, babe. You work nonstop. Enemies need to be taken out. Drink." She pushes the fresh martini in my direction. I was so wrapped up in being annoyed that I didn't realize the bartender had placed it down in front of us. "So, he probably has a tiny pecker, and he's trying to ruin your career?" she asks, scrunching up her face when she finally understands the issue.

"Never mind about his pecker." The mere thought of it has my body craving the feel of him inside of me again. "If he has his way, I'll be without a job very soon."

"Maybe he wants you to work." She coughs and laughs slightly. "Under him."

"Did you start drinking before I got here?"

She shrugs with a devious little grin. "You were late. I couldn't wait any longer."

My phone chirps in my purse, but I ignore it. "He won't leave me alone. He's pursuing me. If word gets out that I slept with him, my career and reputation will be in the toilet." My phone goes off again, and I reach in my purse to turn off the ringer and catch a glimpse of the messages.

Antonio: Meet me tonight

Antonio: You know the room... I'll wait for you.

Who the hell does he think he is? I made it quite clear that nothing more would happen.

"Is that him?" she asks, leaning forward and trying to peek into my purse as I close it.

"No."

"Don't lie to me, Lauren. He's staring at you with hungry eyes."

"He can keep looking, Tee." I grab my glass off the bar and steal a glance in his direction. She describes his look perfectly. His eyes are piercing, longing, and full of need. Slowly he strokes his lower lip and stares at me. As the vodka slides down my throat, he licks his lips and I falter. Choking on the martini, I feel my eyes water and block out the view of him.

"Jesus." Tara starts to pound on my back. "Get your shit together, woman. I've never seen you like this."

After I cough enough to finally gasp for air, I wipe my eyes and blink away the tears. "I'm a wreck."

"Shit is the truth. So, tell me more. You slept with him. Did you know who he was?"

Patting my chest, I try to push down the cough that is sitting deep in my throat. "No. He lied about his name. I didn't know or else I never would've slept with him."

"He lied?" she asks with big eyes, clutching her chest. "Why?"

"He said it's just something he does." I sigh and slump over the bar, rubbing my finger against the rim of the glass.

"Did he know who you were?"

I glimpse in his direction and feel my cheeks heat when I catch his eyes. "I lied about my name too, but I keep wondering if he did it on purpose."

"You lied, too?" She gawks at me and smacks herself in the face lightly. "I thought we stopped doing that shit in college."

I hadn't lied about my name in years, but that night it felt right. "I know." I shake my head, laughing slowly, a little ashamed to admit I reverted back to our college behavior.

"So…" She brings the glass to her lips and gulps it down before wiping her mouth. "I assume this could get messy?"

"Ugh," I groan. "So much worse than messy."

"I know I'm not a business gal, but explain it to me. How can a romp in the sack lead to such catastrophe?"

"Gal?" I ask, gaping at her. "What decade are we in?"

"Just answer and stop being Ms. Know-it-all."

"There's a clause in my contract that if Interstellar is purchased by another company, I'll receive a big pay day. It's called a golden parachute."

"Better than a golden shower." She giggles, and clearly, the alcohol has clouded her filter. "Sorry. It's not funny."

"Jesus." I scrub my hand down my face. I need serious Tara. But instead, I have shit-faced and playful Tee.

"Okay." She straightens and pulls her lips into her mouth, wiping her smile away. "You're going to be rich, but your career will be ruined?"

I don't have to look to know he's still staring at me. I can feel it. I need to not let him know how he affects me. I'm sure from where he sits, I'm showing just how much agony he has me in. I need to pull up my big-girl panties and throw on my Wonder Woman cape and brush him off. Him and his beautiful "pecker," as Tara would call it. "It's built into my contract to make Interstellar less desirable. The cost to buy out my contract is so large that it should make Cozza run away, but with the new invention about to become public, they're chomping at the bit to take us over."

Her eyebrows draw together, and her lips scrunch. "I don't see the problem here."

"If word got out that I slept with Cozza's CEO and made twenty million off the deal, how would that look?" I ask, quirking one eyebrow and crossing my arms in front of my chest.

She gasps loud enough that half the bar looks in our direction. "Oh, shit!"

"Yep."

She scoots her stool closer, leaning in, and her eyes darting around the bar. "I'll really kill him for you. I don't see any other way out of it."

I cover my mouth to hide my smile. "Thanks for the offer, but I think that would just draw more attention."

"Offer is always there. I'd go to prison and go lesbian for you." She smiles, glancing toward Antonio before looking back at me. "He really is an asshole if he did this shit on purpose."

"I know. I want to believe it was innocent." I fist my hands tightly in my lap. "But I feel like someone is trying to ruin me, and Antonio is just one step on the ladder to my demise."

"Who else is messing with you? One more of these bad boys—" she lifts her martini in the air "—and I'll become a serial killer for you."

"Down girl." I laugh. Tara always brings me back to earth and helps make light of every situation. "I'll handle them all."

"Is Trent being an asshole too?"

"He's being the number one asshole. I don't want to talk about him, though."

She hops off the barstool and holds up her finger. "Hold that thought. I have to visit the ladies' room."

My belly flips because I'll be alone with him so close. Maybe he won't take the opportunity to talk to me. A girl can hope, right? "Hurry, Tara. Don't leave me here with him over there."

"Just glare at him," she says, rubbing my back. "Drink and glare. Show him you're mad, and he'll stay put."

"Yeah," I say sarcastically. "I'm sure he'll stay over there."

She walks away, keeping her eyes glued to Antonio as she strolls toward the bathroom. I glance in his direction, glaring at him as I take a sip of my drink, but I don't let my eyes linger. I sit up a little straighter as I down my martini and stare at the television screen to the right that's showing mindless chatter from CNN and the next overhyped news story.

I won't allow myself to look in his direction. Looking means interest, and I most certainly am not into him. Sleeping with the enemy is not me. I won't be the victim, and I won't let Antonio be the predator, slowly stalking me to ruin my life for a small piece of ass.

"Lauren," he says in a low, sultry voice from behind me...that accent doing wicked things to my insides.

I don't turn around, just toss back the last bit of liquid courage left in the glass. My face tingles and my legs feel like jelly, and I'm thankful that the stool's underneath me so I don't collapse.

My heart pounds in my chest so wildly I'm worried he'd hear if it were quieter in here. "I'm busy." I keep my eyes forward and don't dare turn around. He sits down, uninvited, and I curse Tara for leaving me alone. "That seat's taken."

"Not at the moment." He sets his drink on the bar and faces me, his legs caging me in. "We need to talk."

I motion to the bartender, and I point to my drink and pray it comes quickly. "No, we don't."

"Listen..." He touches my hand, and although I want to pull away, I close my eyes instead and relish his touch. "I don't know what you're thinking, but you need to know that I had no idea who you were. I didn't set you up. If anything, the entire thing could blow back in my face too." His fingers sweep across the top of my hand, sending tiny shock waves through my system.

"How?" I turn toward him. "How exactly could you come out looking bad in this entire situation, Antonio? I've never heard a male CEO being accused of fucking their way to the top and earning millions. It happens every day to women in business, but never to men. So, explain to me exactly how you're going to be ruined?"

He continues to rub my hand. "I'll agree there's a double standard, but in no way will I let this ruin you."

"Are you going to drop the bid for Interstellar?" I feel a moment of hopefulness that maybe he has had a change of heart.

"Will you spend another night with me?" He grins, bringing his eyes to mine.

I snatch my hand away. "Absolutely not. Go back to your seat before my friend comes back." I scan the room but don't see Tara anywhere.

Antonio invades my personal space and brings his face close to mine. "It's not over between us, Lauren. I'll let sleeping dogs lie, but one way or another, I'll have you and your company."

"You're a dreamer."

He leans forward, his chest nearly flush against mine and whispers in my ear, "The only thing I dream about is hearing you moan my name again."

I squeeze my eyes shut and try to ignore the ache between my legs. "Just go," I say in a defeated voice because no matter how hard I want to deny it, he affects me.

He brushes the hair off my shoulder and touches his lips to my neck. "Nothing tastes sweeter against my lips than you," he murmurs against my skin.

"Not even owning Interstellar would taste as good?" I squeak and curse myself silently for the girlish sound to my voice.

"Nothing."

I can feel his smile against my flesh. "Please leave me alone, Antonio."

"For now," he says, backing away and straightening. "I'll let you get back to your friend."

"Excuse me," Tara says, sliding back onto her stool. "We're kind of in the middle of something." She looks at me and smiles.

"I'll let you ladies get back to your night," Antonio says, grazing my back with his palm as he starts to walk away. "We'll talk soon, Lauren."

"Is he gone?" I ask, frozen in place and staring at Tara.

She looks over my shoulder. "Yes. He's walking out the door."

I gasp for air because I'd been trying to control my breathing with him so close. "Fucker," I hiss.

"That looked so damn sexy across the room." She smirks and picks up her martini. "Sexy as hell, in fact. It's too bad he's our enemy."

My eyes widen. "Were you watching us?"

She licks her lips and wipes the corner of her mouth with her finger. "I walked out, and he was just getting up, so I thought I'd give you a minute to tell him off."

"Thanks," I say in a snarky tone.

"When he bent down and kissed your neck... Girl, I had to fan myself, but I marched right over to rescue you."

I drag my hand down my face to stop myself from reaching out and smacking her for putting me through that. "I needed it," I say into my hands.

"You looked pretty fine to me. Your face was all red, your eyes were closed, and your lips were parted. I thought you might spontaneously combust right there in your seat."

"Shut up." I laugh and smack her arm playfully.

"Right. Right. Figured as much." She laughs. "He's hot though, Lauren. Like seriously off the charts, ripping my panties off, drop-dead gorgeous."

"Let's change the subject...please," I beg.

"Not a chance, my friend." She winks. "Drink up because we have some plans to make."

That's code for trouble. Tara already has the wheels spinning, and I figure by the time I crawl out of here, she'll have a way for me to make them all pay. I'm game for anything, especially saving my company and my name.

Chapter 9

I wipe my palms down my perfectly pressed black skirt, glancing around the launch pad and soaking in the excitement around me. There are so many people waiting to watch our new engine soar into the sky that I can barely breathe. Maybe they're here to watch us fail, but I push that thought aside and try to rein in my thoughts and control my anxiety.

I know the engine will work. If Trent, although he's an asshole, says it's perfect, I have to believe him. His reputation is on the line as much as Interstellar's. If the engine crashes and burns, literally and figuratively, so does his future in this industry.

"Ms. Bradley," a reporter from the most watched cable news network calls to me from the press area.

I look in his direction and give him a smile. He's beautiful with his silver hair and chiseled jaw. I've always had a thing for him, often watching the news just to catch a glimpse of his pretty face, even though he often takes on hard hitting issues. Sometimes when I want to tune out the world, I put the television on mute just to have him in my living room.

"Yes." My smile widens as he pushes through the crowd, and his gaze lingers on my calves. "It's nice to see you, Carter."

"It's completely my pleasure." The words roll off his tongue before his lips turn up in a sinful smirk. "Would you be interested in sitting down for an interview later today?"

I want to leap across the red velvet rope and do the interview now because escaping the craziness around me doesn't sound like a half-bad idea, but I remain firmly planted in my spot. "I'd be honored, but let's see how the test goes."

His ice-blue eyes bore into me. "Are you expecting it to fail?"

I shake my head, knowing it'll go off without a hitch...or at least, I pray to God it does. "No, sir. I don't want to promise something I'm not sure I can deliver. When the engine works perfectly, and it will, there will be a lot to do afterward."

His face softens, and the devilish smile returns to his handsome face. "I just need ten minutes."

I've fantasized about getting Carter alone for ten minutes. I figured I'd climb his six-feet-seven-inch frame with the skill of an Olympic gymnast and have him ravage me in record time. There'd be nothing slow about our first time as I memorized every inch of his muscular body.

"Ms. Bradley," Carter says, pulling me out of my perverse fairy tale.

My face heats as I clear my throat. "Find me after the press conference, and if I have time, I'll give you ten minutes."

His smile widens. "I look forward to it."

I finger the necklace around my neck and wonder if the blush has remained contained to my face, because my skin feels like it's on fire. Carter is more handsome in person, and I'm sure ten minutes alone with him will make me a blubbering mess of verbal dribble.

He disappears back into the crowd of reporters currently vying for my attention, but there's no more time left for idle chitchat. We're under thirty minutes until takeoff, and I have an entire team to meet with and verify that everything is on track and in working order.

I'm halfway across the tarmac, the airplane fashioned with our new engine sitting proud and ready to show the world Interstellar is no longer number two, when a hand wraps around my arms and hauls me backward.

"Lauren," he whispers as his chest is pressed against my back.

The way he says my name sends chills down my spine and steals my breath. For a moment, I forget we're in public and that he's the enemy. I crave his touch, his warmth, and his calmness, but then my sanity returns, and I start to pull away.

"I need to see you tonight," Antonio whispers in my ear.

I spin around on my heels as he releases me, glaring at him. "Antonio." Saying his name leaves an acidic taste in my mouth.

I know he's here for one thing...to watch Interstellar fail. I want so badly to drink him in like I did the night I spent with him before I knew he was my archenemy, but I somehow keep myself grounded in the moment and the realization that he isn't to be trusted.

"I'd appreciate it if you kept your hands off me when we're in public."

The corner of his mouth tips upward. "So, in private..."

I instantly regret my words.

"No," I say quickly and stop him from finishing the sentence. I glance around, but no one seems to be paying us any attention since we're at a distance from the hustle and bustle of the press, public, and Interstellar team. "I can't be seen with you."

"Come to my penthouse at eight. I'll have a car pick you up and bring you in the private entrance under the hotel."

I take a step back and gawk at him. He can't be serious. He was the best fuck I'd had in years, but that doesn't erase the fact that he's trying to steal the company right out from under me. I straighten my back and raise my chin, putting up my sexy-man force field to prevent me from saying yes. "While I appreciate your offer, Mr. Forte, we must keep our relationship inside the boardroom."

"I'll do you anywhere you want." He smirks.

I fist my hands at my sides and grunt my disapproval. "If you'll excuse me, I'm about to crush Cozza—and you, for that matter. Stick around and watch as I top you."

"Baby, you can be in control," he says as I start to walk away. His words do funny things to my insides, and I turn my back to hide my face because I know he'll be able to read me like an open book. "Just be ready at seven thirty when my car picks you up."

I wave him off over my shoulder, but I've agreed to nothing. The man has the biggest set of balls on him if he thinks I'm going to throw myself at him and beg to keep my company. It's not my style, and I haven't made it this long and this far by using sex. I'm not about to start now.

The only way I'll crush Cozza and Forte and send them packing will be a successful test flight, along with finding the loophole that'll have them running for the hills with their tails between their legs.

I avoid turning around and giving him one last glance as he sits on his high horse, still thinking he's in control. I don't feel bad knowing that I'll be pushing my stiletto heel into his chest and piercing what little heart he has within the next thirty minutes. I feel more alive than I have in years, knowing that the company I helped build will overtake him and become the new number one in the aerospace industry.

Trent's standing about thirty feet away from the airplane, staring up at it and stroking his chin.

"Everything okay?" I ask as I come to a stop next to him and look up to see what has his attention.

"It's perfection," he says with a softness that's so unlike him. "I actually created this magnificent beast."

"I always knew you could do it." I turn my head and gaze at the man I once thought I loved. For a second, I remember how good things were before he became a creep but a necessary evil I put up with for the sake of the company.

"I did it for you, Lauren."

I can't hide my expression as I stand here surprised by his answer. Trent isn't a giving person. He's all about number one, and I don't believe for a moment that he invented the engine for me. It was purely ego.

"Let's not kid ourselves, Trent. We're never going to be a couple again. You created that." I point toward the rocket but keep my facial expressions soft so I don't set him off before the launch. "Because you could. You're the most brilliant man I know when it comes to technology, but not when it comes to relationships. Let's not ruin today with an argument. There's too much good today to taint it with our past."

"Ms. Bradley," Cassie interrupts.

I almost breathe a sigh of relief at her timing. "Yeah?"

"It's time for you to address the shareholders and board of directors before it's go-time." She smiles, and her gaze wanders along the exterior of the airplane as it reaches toward the clouds.

"Thank you, Cassie. It's time to get this show on the road. It's the day we've all been waiting for, and there's no need to delay it any longer than necessary. Is your team ready, Trent?"

"They are. We're right on schedule, and all systems are a go," Trent says before I turn and follow Cassie toward the entrance to the hangar that's filled with Interstellar investors and other VIPs.

I've been to events like this for other companies, and I've never seen so many people in attendance. The buzz almost makes me high and amps up the excitement that I can already barely contain. Every news channel and newspaper in the country, maybe the world, is talking about our test flight and how it could change the future of aviation and space exploration.

"Ah, Ms. Bradley," Mr. Grayson welcomes me as I enter the VIP shareholder area.

I slide my hand into his as he holds it out to me. "It's so wonderful to see you again so soon, Mr. Grayson." I can't contain my smile when I speak.

He gently pats the top of my hand. "I knew from the moment you took over that you'd do amazing things."

My insides warm at his compliment. "Thank you, sir."

The glow from his kind words is quickly dimmed as I think of my father. Having him by my side today would've made everything that much sweeter. I had no bigger cheerleader than him, and the only thing that even came close to his love for me was his infatuation with the stars.

"Enjoy today. It's rare for any CEO to accomplish something so profound. I've been around long enough to know how precious and far between days like today are."

"Yes, Mr. Grayson. I'm soaking it in and memorizing every moment."

"That's my girl," he says with a soft smile. "Now go kick some ass."

I chuckle at his use of words. He's usually so proper that hearing profanity roll off his tongue somehow makes me happy.

Josh is waiting for me a few feet behind Mr. Grayson, staring at the plane much the same way I had just a few minutes before. He's buzzing with excitement. Well, as much buzzing that Josh can do without making it too obvious. He's not much for outward expression and over-the-top enthusiasm, but if I didn't know any better, I'd say Josh was giddy.

"It's finally here." Josh turns to me and lets out a sigh of relief. "We're going to kill it, Lauren. Kill. It."

"We've got this." I playfully nudge his shoulder.

Josh rose within Interstellar just after me, and we started only a few months apart. We both knew we wanted to change the company. Hell, we wanted to change the world, and now we are finally achieving our goal.

"If everyone could please take their seats," I announce as I move toward the podium with Josh at my side.

I take a few deep, cleansing breaths as I walk up the steps with my back to the crowd. The sun glints off the metallic surface of the plane's exterior, sparkling like a diamond, demanding attention.

The mahogany podium is still and cold under my fingertips as I stare out into the crowd. The top Interstellar executives and investors are in the few front rows, and behind them are other industry guests and media.

Standing in the very back with folded arms and a cocky grin is Antonio. His eyes are hungry, appraising, and scorch my flesh with his sweeping, intent gaze. Heat creeps up my chest, and I fidget from one foot to another to avoid fanning myself. I will not let him know the way he affects me.

Clearing my throat, I put on my best game face and wait for the crowd to settle. Their voices wane, but the clinking of last-minute preparations drone on behind me in the distance.

"Thank you for being here." I smile wide and swallow down all the nervous energy that's building inside. "Interstellar and I are thrilled for each and every one of you to be here today. Today, with the launch of our newest invention, we'll forever change the landscape of travel around the world and into the heavens."

My eyes catch Antonio just as he licks his lips. I suck in a breath, pulling back from the microphone just in time for it not to be heard by everyone in attendance.

"The engine will allow the human race to reach deeper into space than we've ever been able to before, without a single drop of fuel or an endless supply of energy. Nothing like this has ever been developed—though many have tried and failed—until now. We welcome you to watch the marvel known as the Mercury engine and see for yourself the power and speed that will greet interstellar travels from this moment into the distant future. Please hold all questions until the test flight has taken place. There will be a press conference immediately following the successful launch. Buckle up, ladies and gentlemen, you've never seen a takeoff quite like this."

The crowd erupts as I step back, and I take a moment to soak everything in. The people. The excitement. The energy. The moment before something so amazing is unveiled and seen for the first time. There's nothing quite like it. I'm not sure I'll have another moment like this in my career.

I avoid eye contact with Antonio as I come down the stairs and take a seat next to Josh. We glance at each other with wide eyes because everything is hinging on what's about to happen. Not just our careers, but the very existence of Interstellar. If Trent's engine has any type of massive failure, Cozza will be able to snap up the remaining shares of Interstellar, and we'll cease to exist.

My leg is shaking as the jet slowly rolls down the runway away from us. I can barely contain the excitement and nervousness that are coursing through my body. I place my hands on my skirt and try to calm my legs before everyone in the crowd mistakes my excitement for fear or uncertainty.

When the jet has taken its position at the end of the runway, ready for takeoff, I give the signal to the launch team. It's now or never. The giant body starts to roll forward slowly, and my fingernails dig into the flesh just above my kneecaps as I lean forward with the rest of the crowd.

There's no sound except for the massive engines as they roar to life as the jet picks up speed. The air around me evaporates, and I hold my breath, praying we didn't miscalculate a single thing.

Unlike a normal plane, the one fitted with the Mercury engine only needs a third of the runway to gain enough speed to take off. Not only does it use no fuel, it's faster than anything else out there today. Ours puts the now defunct and out of commission Concorde to shame.

People clap wildly as the front wheels lift off the ground sooner than anyone expects. Almost effortlessly, the entire body of the jet lifts off the ground and ascends toward the clouds. Not wanting just to show that it can and does work, the pilots push it to the limits, rocketing the engine toward the sky at a seventy-degree incline that would make most people sick, but not trained professionals like them.

The pilots asked for permission, wanting to show the ability of the engine, and there was no way in hell that I'd say no. I wanted not only to show the world what we'd accomplished, I wanted to rub it in Cozza's face that we'd made the biggest, meanest, cleanest engine in the world.

I take a moment, turning slowly in my chair to gaze at Antonio. For once, he's not staring at me. He's gaping at the jet, taking in the wonder of the Mercury engine.

And with any luck, his plan is crumbling.

Chapter 10

I haven't come down from the high of watching the engine work perfectly, the media buzz afterward, and the knowledge that Antonio is hopefully crying in his Cognac somewhere in the city. I don't want this day to end, so I stay until there's nothing but quiet surrounding me. I'm the last person in the office building besides the nighttime cleaning crew.

"We did it, Daddy," I say to no one before sipping the last drop of champagne from my glass. The celebration after the press conference was enormous. Thankfully, Antonio was nowhere to be found as we toasted to the future of Interstellar and the Mercury engine. "You're not here to see it, but what we did..." My voice trails off as tears begin to fill my eyes, and I wipe them away. "I wish you were here." There's a bittersweetness to everything that's happened today because my father missed it.

He would've been jumping for joy, always my biggest cheerleader. He did get the all clear to reenter the space program after he fully healed, but he declined because he didn't want to leave me alone if something would happen to him on a mission. I never forgot what he gave up for me, and I think in this moment, he's smiling down at me, wrapping his arms around me.

"No tears," he'd say to me if he could. "Revel in the moment that you're going to send people further into the heavens than we ever thought possible."

I set the glass down and collect myself, allowing only a few minutes to grieve his absence before heading for the elevators.

All night, I've successfully avoided Antonio's driver and the persistent calls that went on for more than an hour. Blowing Antonio off wasn't easy, but it sure as hell was satisfying.

The elevator dings with each floor, growing louder the closer it comes to the lobby. I almost float out of the elevator and into the large, glass space that leads to State Street. If I weren't so high on the events of today and buzzing from the champagne, I would've seen the black Escalade parked in front with Antonio leaning against it before I walked outside.

"Lauren." He pushes off the car as I try to veer to the right to avoid him, but he steps in front of me. "Wait."

I gaze into his blue eyes and try not to lose myself in them. "I'm tired, Antonio. It's been a long day."

Why does he have to be so damn hot?

"I just want to congratulate you."

I gawk, completely caught off guard. "Thank you," I say with my mouth slightly agape. "Now, if you excuse me." I start to walk away, proud that I was able to leave before something happened...again.

I know I sound bitchy, but for the love of all that is holy, I can't let this man get under my skin. Under any other circumstances, I'd be in the back of the Escalade, kicking his dress pants down his legs. I'm trying to remain strong, using my bitch meter as the only means to try to chase him away.

"I still plan to takeover Interstellar."

His words turn my insides cold, and I turn on my heel and stalk back toward him. "Excuse me?" I tip my head, wondering if I heard him wrong.

"I'm moving forward. Nothing's changed. I want Interstellar more than I ever have before."

Folding my arms in front of my chest, I glare at him. "You want Interstellar, or is it me you're really after?"

He tucks a hand in his pocket, giving me a cocky smile. "Funny you should ask that. I have a proposition you may be interested in hearing."

I should walk away. Hell, I should run. There's nothing he could say or do that would make me want to agree to any proposition he's offering. "You think I want to hear anything you have to say?"

One of his hands slides around my waist, pulling me close. "It's more about you feeling what I have to offer."

My breathing hitches from the contact and his words.

His cologne. His warmth. His hardness. Everything about him makes the very air around me evaporate. "Antonio." I don't know if I'm warning him, but by the sound of my voice, it comes out almost like a moan. Way to go, Lauren.

"Come with me, and I'll explain. It may be the only way for you to save your company."

I look around the streets, and they're quieter than usual. There's no security to usher him away, but then again, there are no witnesses to yet another display of inappropriate behavior on the part of Mr. Forte. "I..."

He leans forward, cutting me off, and brushes his lips against my ear so only I can hear his sexy words. "Give me one hour. It's all I ask. If I you don't like my offer, I'll have my driver take you right home with no strings attached."

"One hour. After that, you'll never contact me again. Deal?"

"It's a deal, Ms. Bradley." With his hand on the small of my back, he ushers me inside the waiting Escalade.

■ ■ ■ ■ ■ ■ ■ ■

I tap my finger against the champagne glass I'm holding as I gaze out of the expansive windows of Antonio's penthouse. I've been here twenty minutes, and he still hasn't told me about the offer. It must've all been a ruse to get me back in bed.

"Come sit, please." He taps the cushion on the couch. The very one that we fucked on the night Lou and Elizabeth met. It seems like a lifetime ago and something I wish I could take back.

Slowly, I move toward the sitting area, taking a seat out of arm's reach from him. "You have forty minutes left. Get to the proposition before you run of time."

Antonio undoes his cuff links, tossing them onto the coffee table before rolling up his sleeves. I salivate at the movement as each muscle of his arms ripples. "Cozza has no plans to drop the takeover of Interstellar."

"You've told me this already." I cross my legs, trying to calm the slow burn that's settling there while I watch him undo a few buttons on his dress shirt.

"I have the ability to call it all off," he says nonchalantly.

"Do it, then."

He clicks his tongue before grinning. "I've always been a winner, Ms. Bradley. I won't freely give up my plans without getting something in return."

My head jerks back. He seriously wants me to fuck him to get Cozza off our backs? "You can't be serious."

"It's either you or Interstellar. I prefer to have you in my bed."

"I'm not a whore, Antonio." My lip snarls at the insinuation that I'd ever agree to his deal. I should've known his proposition would involve me spreading my legs again, but I wasn't expecting it from a man of his caliber.

"Don't make it sound so tawdry. All I ask is for one weekend. At the end of the weekend, if you hate my guts, I'll call off the takeover and be on my way. But..."

"But, what?" I don't even know why I'm still sitting here listening to his crazy proposal, but I am because I love my company and, well, that Antonio is fucking amazing in the sack doesn't hurt either.

"But nothing. Forty-eight hours is all I ask."

Antonio Forte has guts. I'll give him that. Not many men would proposition someone, especially their enemy. If I leaked any of it to the press, it would end his career, but the bastard knows mine would end as well.

"No. We had one night together and it was okay, but I'm not repeating it." I can feel the heat creeping up my neck at the lie, but hopefully my shirt hides my body's betrayal.

"I'll sweeten the deal." His blue eyes twinkle as his cocky, self-assured smirk grows.

I set my glass down on the table, ready to walk out on the entire conversation. This is ludicrous. I don't even know why I agreed to come here and give him an hour of my time. Because he does magic things with his tongue and cock, Lauren.

As I stand, he says, "If you agree to a weekend and stay for the entire time, I'll give you the name of the mole in your company."

I lower myself slowly back onto the couch. Besides sending Cozza for the hills, I want to know who leaked our invention more than anything in the world. I want to have a chance to ruin their career much like they almost ruined my company. "You know who it is?"

He nods and leans back, placing his leg on top of his knee and relaxing against the couch. "The only way you'll ever find out is to give yourself to me freely this weekend."

"That's dirty and verges on blackmail."

"It's not blackmail. I would never ruin your career over what happened between us, but if you want to know who your real enemy is, then say yes."

What a giant clusterfuck. I'm screwed no matter what I do. If I give in and word gets out, it would kill my career. If I don't say yes and don't allow him to use me for a weekend, I would likely be giving up my company and never bring the mole to justice.

I feel trapped, and it's not something I deal with well. I've never allowed myself to be backed into a corner like this, and I don't want to blurt out an answer and regret it later.

"I need the night to think about it." My stomach churns as soon as the words leave my mouth. I should tell him to go to hell, march out the door, and never look back.

"You have twenty-four hours until the deal expires. After that, I'll move forward with the acquisition of Interstellar, and the mole will remain forever hidden."

"You'll have your answer by close of business tomorrow, Antonio. If I do agree to this, it's only a weekend and nothing more."

"Was it that bad?" he asks, running his index finger along his bottom lip as my eyes follow.

"What?"

"Being with me? What did you call it? Okay."

I laugh at the serious look on his face. "You were good, but not the best." God, I almost convince myself with the bullshit lie and wonder if he can see right through me.

"Lie to yourself all you want, Lauren, but I was there. I saw how you came, the way you moaned, and can still remember your sweetness on my tongue."

Problem is...so can I.

Sleep doesn't come easily. I spend at least a half hour tossing and turning as I replay the conversation with Antonio over and over again in my head. The nerve of that man to actually bargain sex for information and the very existence of my company. The crazy thing is, I'm actually thinking about saying yes.

Times like these, where I'm stuck with no one to go to for advice, I miss my father most. He'd be a kind ear without judgment, and he'd help me work through the various scenarios and how it could all blow up in my face in a heartbeat.

What would he think of me for even entertaining the deal? His dream was for me to reach the stars. In essence, I will be, or at least others will, because of the Mercury engine. Would he tell me to do it, to do anything to make it a reality? Even if it means selling my soul in order to secure the future of my company and everything I worked so hard to build?

Spending forty-eight hours with Antonio wouldn't be awful. The man is sexy and killer in bed. If he were anyone else, anyone in the world besides the very man who's trying to end my company, I would've already said yes. He and I would work under any other scenario. I could see the chemistry and sex turning into something more, something serious.

I push away the thought of any type of future with him or the fairy tale I'm building in my overtired mind. What in the hell am I thinking? We're nothing. We're enemies and nothing more.

Could I say yes? I want more than anything to keep Interstellar a separate entity from Cozza, and finding out whom the mole is an added bonus.

Then there's Antonio. My life has been so devoid of any type of sexual encounter besides the one-night stand with him that my body is screaming for me to say yes.

It's only a weekend, right?

A weekend of sex. A weekend of orgasms. A weekend of him touching me and me touching him. The ache between my legs answers the question for me. Sliding my hand down my abdomen, I press a finger against my clit, trying to calm the throbbing that has settled at my core.

"Damn," I mumble to myself, closing my eyes and picturing Antonio standing before me naked.

I dip two fingers inside, pumping them in and out, thinking only of him. The way he calls my name, rolling the R as he moans in my ear, sends me spiraling over the edge quicker than I expect.

Antonio Forte is seriously fucking with my head.

Chapter 11

Antonio

After watching the Mercury engine take off and everything that Interstellar has accomplished, I knew Cozza could no longer move forward with the acquisition of Lauren's company.

Not as things stand now.

There's no way we'd pull off a hostile takeover in the midst of the announcement of one of the biggest inventions of this century.

But I wasn't ready or willing to give up my time with her. That night, the one when I was Lou and she was Elizabeth, I felt something more than her skin. I had no idea who she was when we met in the bar. Just like her, I didn't realize the massive mistake until she walked into the lobby of Interstellar to greet our team.

Shocked doesn't even begin to describe how I felt in that moment. Of all the women in Chicago I could've slept with, fate pushed us together.

Lauren hates me. The look on her face when I told her about my proposition said it all. But she doesn't understand. She doesn't get why I'm doing this, but then again, she can't.

I don't want just a weekend, I want it all. I want her. I want Interstellar. I want everything. I'm the type of man who's used to getting it too. Even though Lauren acts like she hates me, I see the way her breathing changes, her cheeks flush, and her body reacts when we're close. She keeps her distance, trying to avoid contact because she doesn't want me to know how much I affect her.

But she, much like I, myself, can read people. I don't need her to say the words. Watching tells me everything I need to know. I want two days of the real us, uninhibited, alone, with no outside interference. I don't know what it is about her, but all I know is that I want her and only her.

No woman has ever captivated me before her. Maybe it's the fire in her eyes that has me almost in a trance. The fierceness with which she defends her company is the biggest turn-on. She's the complete package. Hardworking, dedicated, loyal, beautiful, and smart. What man wouldn't be clawing over the back of another to be with her?

"Cancel the meeting this afternoon, and alert the team that the takeover is on hold."

"Are you sure about that, Antonio?" Alesci asks over the phone as I head toward the elevator.

"Yes. I have an important matter to attend to this weekend. We'll see where we're at next week."

"I'll let the team know. They're not going to be happy."

"It's what I want. Make it happen." I hang up just as the elevator doors open.

The only thing I'll be focusing on is Lauren. She can protest all she wants, but I know she's going to say yes. Not only because she wants me, but she'll do anything to save her company, even if it goes entirely against her grain.

A gust of wind hits me as I walk out the front doors of the hotel, reminding me why I hate this city in the winter. The weekend I have planned won't take place here. There's too many people in both our circles that could run into us, and I need a break from the cold spring air. The weekend I have in mind involves very little clothing and a warm ocean breeze.

Calvin, my driver, quickly opens the door so I can escape the frigid air. "Good afternoon, sir." He smiles, seemingly unaffected by the weather before closing the door.

"Afternoon, Calvin. Did you get everything on the list?"

"Sure did." Calvin nods. "Everything is in the back, Mr. Forte."

I had a list of items that were needed for this weekend to go off without a hitch. I wasn't even going to let Lauren go home to get clothes, because she could change her mind, and I don't want to give her extra time to back out of the deal.

"Perfect. Thank you. Interstellar, please."

"Yes, sir." He gives me a toothy grin, looking back at me in the rearview mirror for only a moment before turning his attention to the street.

It's nearly five, and I told her I would come for an answer before the end of business. She may say no. I don't know what I would do if I were in her shoes.

The drive is short, and traffic is minimal for a Friday. "Ring when you're ready, sir. I'll stay close," Calvin says as I climb out of the Escalade and button a single button on my suit jacket.

"Thank you." I head toward the front doors of Interstellar, taking in the majesty of their opulent building on State Street.

I knew from my research that Lauren had a lot to do with their quick rise to second place in our industry. When she took over, she brought Interstellar into the big city and hired the right people to surround her. But she made a critical error. Not everyone is trustworthy, especially when they're greedy and ruled by the almighty dollar instead of loyalty.

"Mr. Forte, it's so nice to see you again." Lauren's assistant turns toward her office door and fidgets from foot to foot. "Is Ms. Bradley expecting you?" She chews the corner of her bottom lip as her eyebrows draw together.

I tuck a hand in my pocket and smile, trying to calm her nervous energy. "She is."

Her eyebrows shoot up. "Oh. Okay. Let me announce you."

"There's no need for that, ma'am. Lauren and I are well acquainted."

"I know." She laughs nervously.

Her response catches me off guard. I lean forward so no one else can hear. "What do you know?"

"You're Lou," she whispers.

I lean back, studying her face and pink cheeks. "You know who Lou is?"

"I know some. I saw your messages on her phone." She glances down at the floor and bounces on her heels.

"Do you know why I'm here?"

"Um," she mumbles.

"It's okay. Whatever you know is fine, but this is our secret. Understand?"

She gives me a firm nod. "Understood, sir."

"I'll show myself in. Please make sure we're not disturbed. Will you do that for me?"

She gives me a wink. "I can do that. No interruptions."

"Thank you," I say, giving her a small wink before heading toward Lauren's office.

I'm here for my answer, and I won't accept anything except yes.

Lauren

My back is turned to the door as I stare out the window, watching the sunshine sparkle off Lake Michigan in the distance. I expect to hear Trent's voice, breezing in like he always does when the person speaks.

"Ms. Bradley."

Antonio.

I close my eyes and take a deep breath, waiting for the door to close before facing him. "Mr. Forte," I say, keeping with formality as I spin my chair around.

"Always a pleasure." He grins with a curt nod as he unbuttons his perfectly pressed suit jacket. "As promised, I'm here for your answer."

I keep my eyes pinned on him as he sits in the chair opposite me. Everything about him oozes power. The chiseled jaw with the perfect amount of five-o'clock shadow. The deep blue of his eyes and the longer-than-should-be-legal-on-any-man eyelashes. Even his lips are divine and perfect for kissing. His suit is expensive, probably a blend of silk that caresses his skin as he walks.

Stop, Lauren. I clear my throat and lean back in my high-back chair, swiveling it around as I take in the sight of him. I'm drawn to him. Damn. More than I should be. But the memories of our tryst don't make it easy to forget everything Antonio has to offer.

"I've given your offer a lot of thought."

I'm stalling. I want to say no. I know I should say no, but there's part of me that's screaming for me to say yes and run away with him.

"Time is running out." He smiles and rubs his fingertips along the leather armrest. "Just say yes, and all your worries could be over."

Easy for him to say. Saying yes could be my biggest mistake ever. Bigger than Trent, and that's saying something. Do I trust Antonio to hold up his end of the bargain? No way. I've been in this business too long to believe a word that comes out of anyone's mouth, especially the man who's trying to take my company right out from under me.

I lean forward, clasping my hands together on my desk and look him straight in the eyes. "Are you willing to put it in writing?"

Antonio moves quickly, grabbing the tablet sitting near me and a pen and jotting down a note. I gawk at him, watching the muscles in his hand move and flex with each stroke of the pen.

When he's done, he scribbles his signature and then pushes the paper in front of me. "There. Are you ready?"

"Ready?" I ask, almost choking as I stare down at his words.

I, Antonio Forte, will put the takeover of Interstellar on hold and reveal the mole inside said corporation if and when Lauren Bradley spends forty-eight hours with me. During this time period, she is entirely mine to use as I wish. She must give herself completely and without reserve. After she's fulfilled her part of the agreement, I will fulfill mine.

Antonio Forte, CEO Cozza Corp.

Use as he wishes? Give myself entirely to him? I'm momentarily dumbstruck at his choice of words. "I need a moment," I say, but when my legs start to press together to calm the burning ache at my core, I know my answer. I lift my eyes to his, and butterflies fill my stomach. "I agree."

"Everything you'll need for the weekend is already in my car. I'll give you a moment to collect yourself, and then you can meet me downstairs." He pushes the pad of paper in front of me. "Sign it too, Ms. Bradley."

I scribble my signature next to his with shaky fingers before he turns the pad and snaps a quick photo.

"We each have a copy. It's binding."

My mouth is dry, but my body is on fire. My mind is going a million miles an hour, and I already regret agreeing to such insanity. But, if nothing else, I can keep him occupied while the rest of my team comes up with a way to stop Cozza forever. Antonio will be too busy with me to move forward with the acquisition of Interstellar.

"I need a few minutes."

"I'll be waiting. The forty-eight hours starts as soon as you're in my car."

I nod and try to swallow, but I can't. Damn Antonio. I want to hate him, yet I can't. He walks out of my office without so much as a second glance.

I stare down at the paper, unable to believe I actually signed it. There's no going back now. I can't. I won't. Interstellar is at stake, and I'll do anything to save it.

"Cassie," I say, pushing the intercom button that's hardwired directly to her desk. "A moment please."

She's through the door before I even take my finger off the button. "What do you need?"

"I'm going to be away this weekend with a..." I pause because how do I explain to anyone where I'm going? "Family obligation. Only call me if there's an emergency. Otherwise, contact Josh if something comes up."

"I can do that," she says, but she's grinning like she knows I'm lying, which she probably does.

"Thank you. I'm going to send out a quick email, and then I'm leaving for the weekend. You might as well go too. It's Friday. I'm sure you have plans."

"I'm just curling up with a good book and a bubble bath tonight." She smiles, and I'm a tad bit jealous. She's going to be relaxing while I'm doing God knows what with Antonio.

After she leaves, I type out a quick email to members of our legal team. I'm giving them until Monday morning to figure out a way to end the Cozza takeover permanently. They've had almost a week to do it. If they don't have a solid answer by Monday, we're doomed unless I can persuade Antonio to walk away forever.

I glance in the mirror, checking my makeup and giving myself a mental pep talk before I walk out of the office with my head held high and my stomach in a tight knot. I don't remember another time in my life when I've been so nervous. I shouldn't be, though. It's not like I haven't slept with Antonio before. But that was when he was Lou and I was Elizabeth. Being Lauren and Antonio complicates everything.

Antonio's waiting at the curb as promised, and the clock officially starts to tick.

Chapter 12

Antonio

"Where are we going?" Lauren looks at the private jet and then back to me as we pull onto the tarmac.

"Away from here and prying eyes."

Her eyes widen, and she starts to breathe heavily. "We can't leave the city. What if someone needs us?"

"The world will not end without us. We're safer if we're far away from here."

"Safer?"

I can see I'm losing her. I complicate everything with my dumb-ass responses. It's almost like I'm speaking in code half the time.

I lay it all out on the table. "Do you want people to see us? Possibly see our faces splashed on the news?"

Her eyes flash with anger. "Fuck no."

"Then we're getting on the plane." I point toward my jet that's gassed up and ready for departure. "And going somewhere warmer and more secluded." I push open the Escalade door, done with the conversation and the questions. She signed the contract, promised that she'd be mine for the weekend no matter what I asked, and she's already balking at the idea of getting on the jet.

Calvin grabs the few bags out of the back as I open Lauren's door and hold out my hand. "I promise you'll like where we're going. I put a lot of thought into this weekend, Lauren."

With hesitation, she slides her hand into mine and slowly steps down on her Jimmy Choo shoes onto the cement. "I shouldn't trust you, Antonio."

Her comment makes me laugh. Trust me or not, we're not going to be doing much more than we've already done. It's not like I'm going to take advantage of her. "Did you like Lou?"

She smiles as we walk toward the jet. "Lou, I liked. You, not so much."

"Then I'll be Lou this weekend if you'll be Elizabeth." I give her a peace offering. I don't mind playing a part and pretending to be an alter ego. Anything to make her happy and more comfortable with the entire situation.

She stops at the bottom of the stairs and faces me. "It's just a name and won't change the way I feel about you. We can't change who we are, Antonio. No matter how much I wish you were really Lou, you aren't and never will be."

But that's the furthest thing from the truth. She's confusing who we are with our careers. My life is not comprised of what I do inside the boardroom. My life is what happens when I step outside, when I allow the world and the things around me to seep into my skin. My accomplishments haven't made me who I am. I've made them mine, but they don't encompass me as a person.

This weekend I'll show Lauren who I really am. I'm not the uptight company builder she thinks I am. There are more layers to me than she can ever imagine. Just as I know there's more to Ms. Bradley than her skintight suit skirts and designer high heels.

"After you." I motion toward the stairs, not willing to argue the fact that she hates me. We'll see what happens tonight, and I'll roll with it from there. I have a sneaking suspicion she'll be putty in my hands by the end of the weekend.

The pilot greets us before we enter the main cabin. "Good evening, sir."

"Good evening. Are we ready?"

He nods and glances at Lauren. "Wheels up in five, and we'll be at our destination in approximately three hours."

"Perfect. Thank you, Adam."

Lauren sits on the banquette that stretches the entire length of the jet, cramming herself on the very end. I don't let it dissuade me and stretch out right next to her.

She inches her legs a little closer to her part of the couch and farther away from me. "You never did tell me where we're going."

"To my private island near Nassau."

"You're taking me to the Bahamas for the weekend?"

"Yeah."

"For a weekend?"

Lauren clearly doesn't understand how to enjoy her status and success. The world will not crumble. Her position within her company will not end if she takes time away. Sometimes we need to step back and savor what we have in order to fully enjoy it.

"I like to get away from everything. Don't you?"

"I don't have time." Her brows furrow. "I always thought I would, but I'm too busy with work."

"Such a shame. This weekend, there's no work. Just relaxation and us."

"I need a drink," she says, turning toward the window as the jet begins to roll down the runway.

Like clockwork, the flight attendant walks into the cabin with a dirty martini for Lauren and a Cognac for me.

Lauren grabs the martini and thanks the flight attendant. After she takes her first sip, she turns to me and says, "Slick."

"I left nothing to chance."

I planned every second of this weekend, down to the drinks and clothing. I wanted nothing to go wrong and took pains to ensure it. My point isn't to use Lauren and discard her, it's to win her over and see if we could possibly have something more.

Have I done this before? No.

Why Lauren? She's the female version of me, driven to succeed no matter the cost. I respect her more than she may ever realize. I know she thinks I want to use her, but it's the furthest thing from the truth.

We sit in silence, sipping our drinks as uneasiness settles in the air. The problem this weekend will be getting her to relax and trust me. I'm only her enemy inside the boardroom, not in the bedroom. It's my job to show her the possibilities of what we could become by joining forces and giving in to what we both want... each other.

Lauren

The trip hasn't started like I assumed it would. I figured Antonio would be all over me within the first hour of our trip. I did sign an agreement that he could use me any way he saw fit for the entire weekend. But surprisingly, he hasn't made a single move.

I take the last sip of my martini and feel a slight buzz from downing it quicker than usual. I'm a nervous mess and questioning my decision-making ability after agreeing to this weekend alone with Antonio.

Antonio sets his empty snifter on the table, and I fully expect him to pounce on me. Instead, he slides closer but keeps some space between us. "I have some rules for us this weekend."

"Rules?" My mind starts going to dark places. Ones I haven't allowed myself to think about for years, fantasies I've had that I never allowed to become realities. The thought of going to those places with Antonio is disturbing. The man already has enough dirt on me to end my career, I don't want to give him any more leverage to use against me in the future.

He slides his hand through his dark hair and gives me a smirk as if he's reading my mind. "First, there's to be absolutely no work or talking about our companies." He pauses.

"I can do that," I say when he doesn't continue. I can go without talking about our companies, but it doesn't mean I have to stop thinking of a way to knock Antonio right off his pillar. "What else?"

"Second, I won't do anything with you unless you agree and give your full consent."

That makes the low rumble in my stomach start to calm just a bit. "Okay."

"If there's anything you don't like or you aren't enjoying, you have to tell me, and we'll stop."

"But," I say, pausing for a moment because I'm suddenly confused. I signed a document saying he could use me and now he's giving me the power to refuse his advances.

Antonio stands and removes his suit jacket. I can't take my eyes off him as he moves with grace, draping the fine silk on the chair across the aisle. He unbuttons his shirt, folding the arms toward his elbows one at a time. My mouth waters, watching his body move and remembering how he felt against me that night.

"Do you know why I wanted you here this weekend?"

"To humiliate me." Why else would he invite me away to his island, alone, with a signed agreement to basically be his whore?

He shakes his head and sits down, but he moves closer this time. "The agreement was just to see how willing you were to come with me, Lauren. The last thing I want to do is humiliate you. My intention is to get to know you better and for you to get to know me as a person and not just your enemy. There's more to me than Cozza, just as there's more to you than Interstellar."

I let his words sink in, but I don't believe anything he said. "So, you're not going to use me?"

He laughs softly. "Not unless you ask me to."

It's my turn to laugh. The last person in the world I'd beg to touch me is Antonio. "This should be interesting."

"Very few women capture my attention, but you have. Completely. From the moment in the bar until now, I haven't been able to concentrate on much else."

"It's only because you want my company, Antonio. Let's not fool ourselves."

"This trip has nothing to do with our work. This is about us, about Lou and Elizabeth, about the chemistry we had together."

Memories of that night come flooding back, and I can't deny that sparks flew when Antonio touched me. But that was before I knew who he was and the fact that he was trying to destroy my entire world. "Had is the operative word."

He raises an eyebrow. "You're not still attracted to me?"

"No." I can hear the betrayal in my voice.

He lifts his hand, gesturing toward my face. "May I?"

"May you what?"

"May I kiss you and see for myself?"

I narrow my eyes. "You're asking for permission?"

"Words can betray, but our bodies tell the real truth."

My body betrays me at every turn when it comes to him. No matter what I say, how much I protest, I know once he kisses me, I'll be a goner.

"Kiss me," I say, because there's no way I'm going to say no. I know if I do, I'm just going to validate everything he believes about my attraction to him.

I can do this, right? I can kiss him without reacting. I can pretend he's unattractive. I'll just picture someone else while he's doing it. I'll pretend the person kissing me is Trent, because the very thought of him touching me now repulses me.

Antonio slides closer until our knees touch. The warmth of his skin seeping through his pants is immediate against my bare knees. I close my eyes, waiting for him to plant his lips on me when my hair starts to move. Opening my eyes, I see he's looking behind me, pulling the pin from my hair that's holding my tight bun in place.

"You need to relax, Lauren. Let your hair down this weekend and enjoy yourself." He tosses the black hair stick to the floor before running his fingers through my hair. His fingertips running along my sore scalp is so divine I almost moan.

His hand slides down the side of my face, cupping my cheek. "You're so beautiful."

I don't respond. I can't.

"Close your eyes," he whispers as his thumb strokes the bottom of my cheek near my mouth.

I do as he asks, sealing my eyes shut and picturing Trent.

I will not let Antonio affect me. I will not let him win.

Trent. Trent. Trent. I repeat his name in my head as the warm body next to me moves closer. My plan is working, the steady stroke of his thumb against my skin isn't sending goose bumps across my skin.

But then I smell him and not Trent.

Trent never wore cologne and never smelled like much of anything. Antonio's spicy, expensive cologne lingered on me for hours after our night together, and I'd never forget the smell or how it intoxicated me.

His warm breath cascades over my lips, mingling with his cologne. My plan is no longer working. All I can feel is Antonio, all I can smell is Antonio. I'm surrounded by him, and he's inescapable.

The softness with which he presses his lips to mine surprises me. There's nothing rushed or hurried in his movement. His hand glides behind my neck and tangles in my hair, softly tugging my head back.

He nips my bottom lip, lightly tugging as he kisses me. Soft and slow at first, almost tender, before becoming more demanding.

My head's spinning like I'm drunk on his scent and the feel of him against my skin to the point that I can barely form a coherent thought. My body and mind, being the traitors that they are, react to him. I moan softly, leaning forward into his kiss and opening my mouth to allow his tongue to dip inside.

His hand gently tugs on my hair, pulling my head back and allowing his tongue to push deeper. Tiny shock waves shoot out from my neck, down my spine, and electrify my skin as he kisses me deeper than before.

My plan not to be affected by his kiss is shot to hell. My body betrays me just as I assumed. Thinking of Trent did nothing to stop my reaction to Antonio. I knew what he had to offer. The softness, the hardness, the seemingly endless orgasms.

I have two choices: give in and enjoy the pleasure he offered this weekend or...

Who am I kidding?

There's the only choice. In this moment, with our lips tangled together, it's the only option that makes sense.

I slide my hand up his legs, gently caressing the hard muscles underneath the soft silky material. I'm going to embrace what I set out to do this weekend.

I promised a weekend of pleasure, not only for him but for me too.

If Antonio wanted to ruin me, he already had enough to do that if he wanted to, yet he hadn't. That counts for something. A single word could have sent everything into a tailspin and had the takeover within his grasp, but he didn't. Why? Why would Antonio refrain from taking the company right out from under me when he had the chance?

"Stop thinking so much," he murmurs against my lips.

I do as he says, pushing everything out of my mind but us. The kiss. The touch. The smell. The sounds. The taste. Everything in this moment is about Antonio and me, with a dash of Elizabeth and Lou.

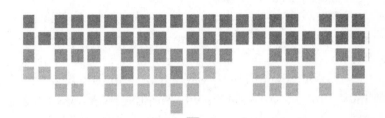

Chapter 13

Antonio

"This is all yours?" Lauren asks at my side as we step foot on the small island I purchased as an escape five years ago.

This place isn't much. Five acres of sand, palm trees, and a single house I use when I need to get away from society and all the trappings. I've never brought another woman here with me. But I couldn't think of a better place to take Lauren that would allow us to get away from everything and everyone in our life and be completely out of the public eye.

"Yes."

She turns in a circle, kicking her bare feet in wet sand after the ocean washes back out before crashing down again. "No one else lives here? A housekeeper, maybe?"

"It's just the two of us and no one else."

The house had been prepared and fully stocked by the two employees who care for the property on my behalf. They were given strict orders not to interrupt us under any circumstances.

"Wow." She glances up at the full moon, backlit by thousands of stars visible in the sky. "I could look at this for hours."

I don't spend nearly enough time on the beach at night, appreciating the beauty and the splendor of the sky without the intrusion of city lights and civilization. The stars twinkle like diamonds on silk, shimmering slightly as we move below. "How about we change into something more comfortable and have a few drinks down here?"

She tilts her head and studies me. "You'd do that?"

I motion to her with my hands. "Come on. We can sleep out here if you want, but I need to get out of my suit and grab a drink."

She walks slowly toward the house, carrying her high heels and glances back at me only once. I regret the language in my contract. I brought her here as a guest, wanting to spend more time with her and see if what I felt that night between us was just sex or something more.

But I laid my cards on the table, and now I must find a way to make her see me as something more than the world's biggest asshole. That title I have down pat, but I want her to see me for who I really am. I worry the hole I dug may be too big for even me to find my way out.

When she steps foot inside the house, she freezes and drops her shoes to the floor.

Maybe I should've told her there's only one bed in my open-air home. Since I'm the only person who stays on the island, there isn't a need for bedrooms. To make the home feel larger than it truly is, there's only one room, like a giant studio apartment. I have a large deck that wraps around the entire home, with doors that fold into the walls, making it feel more like an outdoor space than an actual home.

She turns toward me with narrowed eyes. "There's one bed."

"I know." I grin.

"I snore," she replies quickly. "You won't get any rest if we have to share a bed."

"Lucky for you," I say with an even bigger smile, "I'm a sound sleeper." I'm lying, but then again, so is she. "You can change in the bathroom while I change into something a little more weather appropriate too. We'll discuss sleeping later, but for now, I want to watch the world go by. There's a walk-in closet in the bathroom, and it's filled with clothes picked just for you."

She stares at me, blinking a few times like she's trying to comprehend what I said. I know I spoke the words in English and didn't fuck up the translation, yet she's looking at me like I have three heads. She opens her mouth like she's going to say something, but she snaps it shut just as quickly before heading toward the bathroom.

She glances around the room, running her finger along the table that lines the back of the couch in the center of the room. "I see you have everything planned out, Lou."

I like that she called me Lou. Things were simpler when we weren't ourselves. "I leave nothing to chance, Elizabeth."

"Suave," she mumbles, turning toward me with a smile as she steps inside the all-marble bathroom.

I can't tell if she's happy or plotting my death by that smile on her face. Possibly a mixture of both. She's outside of her comfort zone, but so am I. This has always been my space, my sanctuary from the world, and for the first time in my life, I'm sharing it with another person.

When she closes the door, I undress and put on a pair of loose work-out shorts that I use when I run along the beach. I grab the champagne and two glasses and place the bottle in a bucket of ice before grabbing an oversized blanket. I carry everything down toward the edge of the water where she had stared up in the sky in wonderment.

I've never spent much time wining and dining women, but Lauren deserves as much. She isn't a cheap fuck or a one-night stand. This is something more, or at least I hope it is.

I'm bent over, unfolding the blanket when she steps onto the deck. Slowly, I straighten and take in her beauty in a black and red sarong that's tied over one shoulder. The thin material caresses her body, hugging every inch, and the soft ocean breeze causes the bottom to flutter.

I motion to her, calling her down to the blanket where I'm frozen and unable to move. Her long hair is down, blowing in the wind as if being carried away like my breath. She's stunning. More stunning than she is when she's leading a boardroom, jamming her heel into my chest and trying to maintain her dominance.

There's a softness I hadn't seen before in that dress and barefoot as she pads down the sand toward me. I hold out my hand, praying she'll take it when she's within feet of the blanket.

"You're going to just sit here with me?" she asks, and I can hear the surprise in her voice.

"We can do whatever you want. If you want to drink and stare at the stars, we'll do just that."

With those words, she slides her hand in mine, stepping onto the blanket with a smile. "Thank you."

"Champagne?"

She nods quickly, and I kneel beside her to make short work of the cork. She follows me down, resting on her heels, and watches me.

"I imagine you're bored of this view."

I glance up, taking in her beauty. "I could never grow bored of the beauty in front of me."

Even in the dim light, I see her cheeks turn a bright shade of red as her eyes dip toward her hands for a moment. My fingers push harder against the cork before it pops, shooting into the air. I grab the glasses, holding them between my fingers and pour, but I keep my eyes on her.

Her silhouette is illuminated by the moon, creating shadows across her feminine features. "Thank you," she says as I hand her a glass of champagne before stretching out next to her on the blanket.

"A toast." Holding up my champagne, I take in her beauty as she turns toward me slowly and lifts her glass.

"To the stars, to us, and to this moment amongst the universe."

I clink my glass to hers, our eyes locked as we both take a sip. She's appraising me, trying to figure out when I'm going to pounce. She looks like prey, waiting for the predator to find the weakness and strike, but that's not my intention.

She leans backward on one hand, tipping her neck toward the sky. Even with the champagne still dancing on my tongue, my mouth feels dry. I want to touch her. Lick my way down her neck to her beautiful breasts until she's begging me to bury myself inside her.

"Do you ever want to go there?" she asks, not looking at me when she speaks.

"Go where?" Right now, all I can think about is her body and mine, moving together. There's no room for anything else.

"Going up there." She tips her chin skyward.

"Never. You?"

Being the head of Cozza was more about power and less about moving the human race spaceward. It's what we do, but it's never been my dream to step foot in the outer reaches of space.

She sighs as her eyes move around and settle on the Big Dipper. "Ever since I was a little girl."

Her answer surprises me. How does the dream of a little girl to walk in space turn into a CEO of the second most powerful aerospace company in the world?

"Why haven't you?" I'm intrigued to find out how her dream altered and made her the woman she is sitting before me tonight.

She takes another sip of her champagne before burying the base in the sand deep enough that it'll stay upright. She still doesn't speak as she leans back and settles against the blanket with her hands flat at her sides, staring straight up. I follow suit, repeating her motions, lying down next to her, only inches apart.

"First, tell me why you don't want to go up there. You're the head of Cozza, the current biggest aerospace company, and I figured a man with your status would dream of the stars just like me."

I place one hand on my stomach and inch the one between us closer to her hand. "I was always a science junkie. Figuring out how things work kept me busy as a kid, but the fear of the unknown has always stopped me from even thinking about going into space. I want to help other people get there, but I'm quite happy with my feet on Planet Earth."

"Fear stops a lot of people. We're all afraid of something."

"Why has it always been a dream of yours?"

"Well..." She pauses, and the moonlight glimmers off her eyes as I turn to face her. "It started with my father."

She doesn't say another word, and I don't rush her. Some things take time, and the last thing I want is for her to start closing off walls that seem to be crumbling to little pieces. I turn back toward the starry sky, giving her time and space to speak freely.

I don't know if I've ever lain in such a comfortable silence with another person. The only sound is of the waves crashing against the shore near our feet. The stars twinkle on and off as if fighting over my attention, but there's little room for anything other than Lauren.

"My dad wanted to be an astronaut. He trained for years."

"Did he go?"

"He wasn't able."

I turn my face toward her. "Why not?" I'm genuinely interested in her story and hearing how her father's dreams turned into hers.

Her eyes are glassy, but she hasn't stopped staring toward the sky. "He finished training and was assigned to a specific mission, but..." Her voice trails off.

Oh God. I'm flooded with guilt.

She doesn't have to say another word. I know I've opened up an old wound that she's kept hidden and locked away from the world. We're no longer in business mode or even Lou and Elizabeth world. This is Lauren and her feelings for the taking, and she's spilling them to me, or at least trying.

I roll over and prop myself up on one arm, peering down at her. "You don't have to tell me."

She glances at me with a pained smile. "No, I want to tell you. You need to understand why Interstellar is so important to me."

I nod and remain silent.

Her eyes slowly slide across the sky, not focusing on one particular area. "A few weeks after he finished his official training, there was a terrible accident."

"I'm sorry," I say, interrupting her.

"Don't be. It wasn't your fault." She smiles softly at me, and the ball that had formed in my stomach starts to loosen. "It was my parents' date night. Every Friday, they'd hire a babysitter to look after me, and my dad would take my mom out to dinner and dancing. I never minded because I thought of Mindy, my babysitter, like an older sister. We'd play dress-up, and she'd put makeup on me. I loved Friday just as much as my parents did."

I can imagine her as a child, with her long hair, prancing around in her mother's shoes, covered in too much red lipstick and blue eyeshadow, much like my nieces do when my sister allows them.

"But then a car crossed the center line and struck them head on. My family shattered that day, along with my father's dream."

I've never dealt with the loss of a parent. Mine are still at home in Italy, probably arguing over what to have for dinner or some other mundane thing. They drive me crazy at times, but I can't imagine not having them in my life, especially as a child.

"The police said my mother died instantly, but my father survived."

I don't know what to say in this moment, so I don't speak. I can't say that I'm thankful her father survived because there's still the sadness at the loss of her mother. I can't imagine being in love with someone and having them die by my side in the blink of an eye. The man had to be broken, not physically, but emotionally, with no way to ever repair the hole that had been left in his family.

"He broke his back, and the healing process took a long time. He was eventually cleared to reenter the space program, but he declined."

"He did?"

"Yes. He didn't want to leave me behind, Antonio. He always worried about me, never himself. He could've touched the stars like he always dreamed and left me with my grandparents, but he chose to stay and be there for me. It took me years after his death to get over the guilt that he gave up his dream for me."

"Sometimes dreams are just that...dreams. Just because he never stepped foot in space doesn't mean he gave up his life, Lauren. Men are simple creatures. At times, we can be self-absorbed, but when push comes to shove, we're loyal and protective."

She giggles softly and turns, propping herself up and staring me straight in the eyes. "It took me a lot of years to figure that out. I meant more to my dad than his fanciful dream to touch the heavens. I was the last bit of my mother he had left, and he couldn't stand to part with me, even for a few weeks up there."

"I would've made the same choice as him. I think most men would in his shoes."

She glances down to where our hands are almost touching in the open space between us. "He and I would lie under the stars like this and talk. That became his new Friday night ritual as soon as he could walk again. He'd tell me that my future was up there and pushed me toward where I am now. I became the head of Interstellar because, even though I was too afraid to go into space myself, I wanted to make the dream come true for so many people like my father. I want to allow people to go further, deeper than we've ever been able to go before.

Every day when I go to work, I picture my father cheering me on, propelling me toward my destiny."

And I'm the asshole who's trying to take it all away from her. Not only is Cozza attempting to take her company, but she knows that she'll no longer be at the helm, and in a sense, I'd be killing her dream as well as her father's.

"You've achieved it."

"Not yet, Antonio. The engine's done, but it hasn't carried a human beyond the moon yet. Once it's done that, I'll feel like I've fulfilled my father's dream. Not a moment sooner."

"You've achieved more than I ever thought possible, Lauren. More than I've ever dared to dream."

She smiles and shakes her head. "Oh, please. You have a giant team of researchers that have been working on a similar engine, I'm sure."

"Yes, but I've never found the right combination of people to make it a reality. Never in a million years would my team have thought up something so simple, yet so perfect. They're too busy studying dark matter as a means of propulsion and trying to solve the riddle of how to stop it from destroying the craft with the chain reaction."

She smiles brightly, knowing exactly the type of stupidity I'm talking about when it comes to dark matter. "My team is pretty impressive."

"It takes a great leader with enough knowledge to push their people to achieve such greatness."

"Why, Antonio, if I didn't know any better, I'd think you're impressed and maybe a little jealous."

The lightness in the air between us makes me hopeful. I scoot my body closer, placing my hand on top of hers. When she doesn't recoil or pull away, I know I have her.

"I'm very impressed by you," I say, reaching out and tucking a flyaway strand of her hair that's been blowing in the breeze. "I wouldn't have brought you here if I weren't."

"Come on. I'm sure you bring plenty of women here and show them your private island. It's pretty impressive."

It's my turn to laugh. She doesn't understand how far from the truth her words really are. "Besides the caretakers of this island, you're the first person to step foot on this sand besides me since I purchased this little slice of heaven."

"You can't be serious."

"Completely. This is my escape from the world. I come here to be alone and think. It's not my sex palace or used to impress anyone. It's mine and mine alone."

"Why did you bring me here?" she asks with a sigh. "I just don't understand why me."

I push her hair off her shoulder, letting it fall down her back, and rest my hand against her cool, wind-kissed skin. "I felt something with you that night at the W. Do you believe in destiny, Lauren?"

"I don't believe that things happen for a reason. I think we're all just particles, scattered across the universe, and if we bump into each other, we cause a reaction. There's nothing fated about what happens. It's all happenstance and chance."

I slide my hand down her arm, warming her skin with my touch and relishing the feel of her against my palm. "I don't believe a word of that. Out of all the bars in Chicago, you ended up in mine."

"It was mine first, Lou." She smiles.

"Either way. Our paths crossed for a reason."

Her smile fades. "For you to steal my company."

"Maybe you were placed in my life at that moment to push me onto another course. Ever think of that?"

She contemplates my words, blinking at me while chewing on her lip before she raises an eyebrow. "The universe is conspiring against you?"

"Possibly." I move closer and slide my hand up her arm. "Or maybe reminding me of what's really important in life." My fingers trace her hairline on the back of her neck before tangling in her hair.

I lean forward, waiting for her to pull away, but she closes her eyes and gives in to me.

Chapter 14

Antonio

In this moment, under the stars with our bodies intertwined, I can almost believe in fate.

Antonio yanks at the bow of my sarong, exposing my shoulder as his kiss deepens. I wrap my legs around his back as his hardness presses against my core, just his thin running shorts between us. The warmth of his body mixed with the cool ocean breeze sends goose bumps running across my skin and my body wanting more of his heat and flesh against mine.

"Antonio," I moan into his mouth as he starts to pull away. I'm not ready to give him up, to give this up.

"Shh," he whispers back before his lips trail down my neck, nipping the skin near my shoulder. "Don't stop me now, please, Lauren."

"I want you."

He lifts his head, searching my eyes for reassurance that what I said is true. "I need you," he admits with his blue eyes boring into me.

I dig my fingers into his hair and push his face back against my skin. "I'm yours."

My words shock me. I didn't know what else to say when he freely admitted that he needed me. I know he doesn't mean that he needs me to survive or that he needs me to feel whole. I need him, want to feel him against me and lose myself again, much like I did our first night together.

The moment isn't tawdry. We shared something on this beach. I gave him a glimpse into my world. Into my past that I've told very few people about before now. He didn't feel like the enemy, but like a friend with a kind ear and an open heart.

There's nothing rushed in his exploration of my body, and the anticipation is nearly killing me. He slowly slides his hand up my leg, and my body is on fire, longing for his touch. Every inch of me remembers what it felt like to have his body pressed against mine and wants more.

Using his teeth, Antonio pulls my dress down, exposing my breast for his taking. My back arches as if offering myself to him freely, without words. His lips close around my nipple, giving warmth to my flesh.

I crave more.

I need the friction of our bodies rubbing together as he toys with my breast, making me hotter and driving me mad with lust. I try to grind against him, but he's too far away to get enough satisfying contact.

Knowing exactly what I want, he slides his hand down the side of my body until he reaches the hem of my dress. His fingers slip underneath and make a quick ascent to the very place I'm dying for more contact. Lifting his body from mine, he presses his fingers against my clit, and my bottom rises off the sand.

Between the long, slow make-out session on the plane and the kissing here on the beach, I'm ready for him to fill me. I'm not picky at the moment. His hands will do. I remember them well, and the amount of pleasure he can give with only one part of his body is devastating.

He pushes a single finger inside, testing my readiness and toying with me because he knows it isn't enough. A second quickly joins, and my hips begin to move, almost chasing his fingers every time he pulls back.

I whimper when his mouth leaves my breast for a moment to switch to the one he's completely ignored. I close my eyes, letting myself only feel and not think as Antonio drives me closer to the edge. When my orgasm is within reach, he stops.

"Not like this," he says, peering up at me with my breast near his lips. "I need to be buried in you when you come."

I can't deny that I agree. Even if I want to beg for the orgasm, there's nothing better than his thick, stiff cock pummeling into me as I fall over the edge of pleasure.

"Fuck me," I whisper. "I want your cock."

"You drive me wild with that filthy mouth," he says back and moves quickly to remove his shorts. With the waves of the ocean crashing near our feet, Antonio positions himself above me with his cock in his fist and stares down at me. "Say it again."

"Fuck me, Antonio. I need your cock."

His eyes almost roll back in his head as he moans, pumping his stiff dick harder before pressing it against my pussy. My legs fall to the sides, giving him better and deeper access to me. He pushes inside, and my fingernails press into the skin of his shoulders, delivering a small amount of pain as he fills me.

Little is said as he thrusts inside of me. We're face-to-face. Eye-to-eye. Staring at each other in the glow of the moon with the stars twinkling above us. Our bodies fit perfectly and move in unison as if we've done this a million times before.

It's romantic and sensual. I feel so connected to him when I shouldn't. I should detach myself from the moment, but it doesn't matter who we are when we're not here. The only thing that matters in this moment is us.

Antonio

I drift awake with Lauren in my arms as the sun dances near the horizon. Her warm, naked body is intertwined with mine, and I don't dare move for fear of waking her.

I blink away the sleep and think back on last night. Will she wake up and regret anything that happened?

It wasn't quick like the fuck-fest in the hotel. This was slow, almost loving.

Whatever connection I felt with her that night has grown, becoming undeniable after last night.

She shared so much of herself—not just her body, but her soul too. I stare down at her as she sleeps. She's peaceful and delicate as she lies in my arms. I push a tendril of hair away from her face and run my finger along her jaw.

I've never been so absolutely captivated by someone as I am by her. I shouldn't be. I should be trying to ruin her, not win her over.

The dozen companies I've taken over in the past, I've done without even so much as a moment's hesitation. Everything about the Interstellar deal has turned into a mess. The raid was supposed to be quick and effortless, but my team failed to make it happen as promised. On top of it, sleeping with the CEO and falling for her hasn't helped the deal go smoothly either.

"Lauren," I whisper, but she doesn't move. I untangle her from my body and stand before wrapping the blanket around her. I stretch out the soreness from sleeping on the sand, my muscles aching from the hardness and uneven ground.

Lauren still hasn't moved, but I can't leave her out here. The dark clouds in the distance signal a storm is coming straight toward the island. When I lift her into my arms, her head flops against my chest, and she mutters something that I can't quite make out. Her arms fling around my shoulder as her breathing deepens with each step.

Once inside, I place her on the bed and set out to make a pot of coffee and start breakfast for us both. In the excitement and emotion of last night, I forgot to make dinner like I'd planned once we arrived. Eating isn't always on the top of my priorities because business often gets in the way, but this time, it was Lauren stealing my attention and making nothing else matter.

Lauren starts to stir when the espresso pot whistles on the stove, and I move quickly to quiet the noisy bastard before it wakes her. She seems like the type who hasn't slept in since the day she took over Interstellar, always having to be the first one in the office to show she's on top of her game.

More than anything, I want her to savor the weekend. Not just what I have to offer, but what my life is and how it can be hers if she wants to share it. But it still leaves the question of what to do with Interstellar. I promised her that I'd put the takeover on hold and I have, but it won't be on hold forever. I'll need to find a way to make her happy along with the people who work for and with me at Cozza. It's going to be a balancing act and will only work if she sees me for who I really am and not as the man who's trying to kill her dream.

"Good morning," she says from the bed as she stretches underneath the covers.

"Morning, beautiful." I smile softly at her as I pour two glasses of espresso. "Cream and sugar?"

She pushes herself up on her hands, letting the blanket fall from her chest and exposing her beautiful breasts. "Just sugar, please."

I growl softly, trying to maintain my civility when all I want to do is leap over the kitchen island and pounce on her naked body. The memories of last night are vivid. The softness of her body, the wetness she had for me, and the way she moaned my name as she came on my cock. I want it again. I want it forever.

I prepare our coffee, waiting for my cock to soften just a little before carrying it over to her.

She pulls the blanket over her body and smiles weakly. "Thank you," she says as she takes her coffee from my hand.

I sit across from her on the edge of the bed and take a sip. So far, so good. She doesn't seem upset or angry about what happened last night. There's no remorse in her body language, and she hasn't backed away. "Sleep well?"

"I did. I don't remember the last time I slept so soundly."

"The ocean can do that to a person." I smile against the rim of my glass and take in the beauty of her tousled hair and bare face. "It always helps me sleep. It's the rhythm of the waves."

She nods while looking around the house. "I'm so used to Chicago with the sirens and the L."

The large interior seems endless with the sliding glass doors folded into the walls at the four corners. The high ceiling with the Caribbean woven fans keep the space cool without the sterility of air conditioning. It's the ultimate island getaway—peaceful and secluded.

"How did I get in here? I remember being on the beach."

"I carried you in this morning."

I can't read the expression on her face as she stares at me over the rim of her mug.

"There's a storm coming in, but it should pass quickly and then we can have the entire day to have fun."

This time, her face hides nothing. She chews on the corner of her lip, unsure of what I mean.

"We can go paddleboarding or take the Jet Skis out for a little more action."

Her eyebrows draw down, and tiny wrinkles form under her hairline. "You don't want to stay in bed all day?" She's skeptical of me, and I can't blame her one bit for thinking I'm the world's biggest asshole.

"If that's what you want. The day is long, and we can do whatever you wish."

I can't hide my smug smile. I'd like nothing more than to spend the day making love to Lauren, exploring every inch of her body in the sunlight.

"I've never been on a Jet Ski."

"We must fix that. It's a total high."

She leans back against the headboard, holding her espresso, still staring at me warily. "You're the boss this weekend."

I cringe inwardly at the sound of those words rolling off her tongue. "Lauren, we need to talk." I lean over, setting my cup on the nightstand next to her. "We need to get a few things straight."

She places her cup next to mine before clasping her hands in front of her and eyeing me. "I'm listening."

I adjust my body so I'm sitting near her thighs on the edge of the bed. "I brought you here under false pretenses."

She purses her lips. "Such as?"

I exhale and scrub my hands down my face. "Did I want to have sex with you again? Yes." I look her straight in the eyes. "But that's not the reason I brought you here."

"Plotting my death?" She laughs softly.

I place my hand on the blanket over her thigh. "I know I was an asshole when I made you sign the informal contract in your office. I'm not going to make you my sex slave for the weekend. I brought you here so we could get to know each other."

"I know enough about you," she says, glancing down at her hands before bringing her eyes back to mine.

"Will you always hate me?"

"Will you always try to steal my company?"

I glance up and blow out a heavy breath. "Did you feel that between us last night?"

She doesn't speak and give me affirmation that she felt what I did. I know I wasn't the only one of us who felt the spark. The slow burn that only real chemistry and attraction causes.

I realize I'm squeezing her thigh and release my grip, but I keep my hand against her, grounding her to me. "The first night we spent together, I felt it. I brought you here to see if it was real."

"And did you feel it again?"

"I did," I admit, and it's not something I do easily. "Don't feel like I'm going to demand sex. I won't. It's not something I would ever do. This weekend is about us."

"I didn't know there was an us."

"I hope there is."

Her eyes widen. "Why?"

The answer isn't so easy, so I respond the only way I know how. "Has it been easy for you to find someone?"

She shakes her head, her hair skating across her bare shoulder. Her arms slide up her stomach, settling just under her breasts. Complete defensive posture. I'm getting somewhere even if she won't admit it.

"I've never been able to find someone who likes me for my flaws."

"Yeah, there are a lot." She smirks.

"Stop." I grin. This chick has me in knots and panting like a puppy, willing to follow her around. "I can never be myself with anyone. Women always want to be around me for my money or power."

"Must be a hard problem to have," she replies and rolls her eyes.

"I'm sure you have men falling at your feet because of the power you wield."

Her arms inch higher, almost causing her breasts to spill over the blanket. "Men aren't as turned on by a powerful woman. It's hard to keep their man card in check when I have a higher position and make more money."

I want to lean forward and bury my face between her breasts, but I stop myself. "Some men possibly. But a real man isn't as concerned with power and control. There's nothing sexier than a powerful, confident woman."

"Is that why you like me? I think you're using me as a pawn in the takeover."

I rub my face again, wondering if it's a lost cause. "I like you because I can be me. You're not impressed by my position at Cozza or the money I have in the bank. You're just as wealthy and powerful as I am. Maybe, hopefully sooner rather than later, you can like me for me and not what I can do for you."

Her arms drop to her lap, and she sits up, moving closer to me. "I do like you, Antonio. If things were different, if you weren't trying to dismantle my life's work, we could maybe date. I don't know..." Her voice trails off, and she closes her eyes. "It's easy to be with you too."

I touch her hands, cupping them in mine. "I can separate my business life from my personal. What happens in the boardroom has no bearing on how I feel outside. Right now, no matter what's happening back in Chicago, I'm happy. I'm happy you're with me. I'm happy we slept on the sand under the stars. I'm genuinely happy I'm sharing this time with you. Just a guy and girl on a beach for a weekend without anything else to come between us. Can we put our business life away and just enjoy this time we have together in paradise?"

Her head drops forward, and I can't see her eyes. She's quiet but hasn't told me to go fuck myself yet, so I take it as a good sign. The last thing I want is to argue and have a combative conversation at every turn for the next thirty-six hours before we return to the real world.

"I can do that," she says before looking at me. "I can play nice."

"Will you give us a chance? A fresh start." I hold my breath and hope she'll agree. I want this time with her more than anything.

"I will," she says quickly.

For now, I'll accept the little bits of Lauren Bradley that I can get and hope that the tide will change before we step foot off the sand.

Chapter 15

Lauren

With each skip of the Jet Ski over the crest of the wave, I hold my breath and pray I don't fly off the back. Antonio is screaming at the top of his lungs as we skid across the turbulent surface after the thunderstorm had passed.

My ass slams against the seat as we crash down, and my middle slides forward against him. "Slow down!"

"Isn't this fun?" he asks, turning around and glancing at my face before pushing on the throttle and making the Jet Ski go faster.

"No!" I scream in his ear, making sure he hears the panic in my voice. "You're going to kill us."

I know I'm being dramatic, but I'm clinging to him like my very life depends on his flesh for survival. There is a reason I don't do shit like this. It's scary as hell, and I don't feel in control. Maybe if I had my own, I'd be okay. But Antonio is driving like a madman, and I'm powerless to stop him.

When my fingernails start to dig into his skin, he finally slows. "You want to drive?" he asks, pushing his wet hair back and out of his eyes as I unlatch my nails from his sides.

We've only been outside for an hour, and his skin is already darkening underneath the Caribbean sun. Thank God, I slathered myself with sunscreen, or I'd be in a world of hurt later. My Midwestern skin isn't used to this much sunshine especially when it's only spring.

"Can I have my own?"

"Not yet." He leans over, falling into the water near my feet.

All I can see is his bushy brown hair, floating above him under the surface as his arms and legs flex, moving through the water.

The top of the water shines like a thousand diamonds twinkling in the sunshine. The water is crystal clear and the most beautiful shade of turquoise I've ever seen. I can't help but wish I could stay here forever. The warmth and beauty surrounding me make Chicago seem gritty and cold.

"Come in," he says when his head finally pops out of the water.

"There might be sharks," I tell him and glance around, but I see nothing other than a few schools of small fish nearby.

"You've seen too many movies, love. The water's perfect. Take a dip, and then you can drive."

"It's too deep."

I'm stalling, and he knows it. "It's not." He laughs and finally stands upright, and the water barely reaches his waist.

I can't answer right away. I'm too busy gawking at his golden-bronze chest as the water beads trickle down, scattering every which way like a chip on a Plinko board as they move down toward the top of his swimsuit.

"I'm..." I swallow, and the sun feels hotter than it did seconds ago. The sight of his perfectly chiseled, bare chest sends my libido into overdrive.

Memories of last night come flooding back, and my body craves more of him. Will it always be this way with him? When we leave this island and return to our places as enemies in the boardroom, will I ever be able to hate him again? I'll never be able to forget what's underneath that perfectly polished suit. Not after this weekend.

"You need to get wet."

His statement is innocent, but I already am. I can feel the dampness in my bikini bottom. Being pressed up against him as our bodies bounced and crashed together over the waves made everything worse. The friction was a constant reminder of what he could do to me.

I don't respond as I fall into the water next to him, making sure to create a huge wave to splash him. He looks good wet. Hell, he looks good dry too.

When my feet touch the bottom, I bury my toes in the sand and push up. But I didn't account for the delicateness of the string bikini I have on. I have always been a one-piece kind of girl, but Antonio insisted this was the only suit on the property. As my top half met the air, my bikini top stayed below and floated on the surface.

Blinking through the water trickling from my forehead, I know my breasts are hanging out from the look on his face. It matches mine as I gaze down at his bare chest from the Jet Ski.

"Fuck." I try to cover my breasts with my hands, but they're bobbing with the water and making it damn near impossible.

"Don't." He pulls me toward him, pressing his naked chest against mine. "There's no one around to see anything."

The warmth of the sun does feel great without the restriction of the tiny string holding up my breasts and digging into the skin at the base of my neck. In reality, his skin feels even better against me than the sun ever could.

He leans in and kisses me. I close my eyes and relish the feel of his mouth against mine. His hands slide downward before flattening against the small of my back. The waves splash against us, pushing us with their movement, but we never break our hold.

His kiss grows more demanding, nipping at my bottom lip. I open to him, wanting to feel his tongue sweep against mine and taste him once again. My brain goes fuzzy under the warm sun as I inhale the salt air and the scent that's totally Antonio.

If this isn't paradise, I don't know what is. Everything else in the world seems nonexistent. In this moment, I wish it were. There's something so perfect about this place, about us being together, that I'm scared to allow myself to get lost and forget what's really happening back in reality.

I push off his chest, splashing him as I do with as much water as possible to momentarily blind him. "Let's get going," I say, reaching for my top and facing away from him.

He makes his way toward me as he tries to get the water out of his lungs caused by the tidal wave I sent his way. "Where are you running off to so soon? There's no hurry, Lauren."

I move quickly, attaching my top as I head toward the Jet Ski. "I want to drive before it's lunchtime." I don't know what else to say. I'm grasping at straws, but I don't want to lose focus on what the purpose of this weekend really is. It's easy to get lost in the fairy tale with the tropical setting, warm sun, and almost naked Antonio next to me.

I pull myself up, unable to look at his face because I know what I'll see. I can't face him. Not yet. I'm a mix of emotions when it comes to Antonio. One minute I hate him, and the next I'm falling for the man. None of it is fair either. There's no way we could have a future.

Antonio

I lean over her, placing my hands on hers on the handlebars. "Do this." I scoot forward so our bodies are flush. "When you're ready to slow down, just ease up like this." My hand tightens around hers.

"I got it," she says, wiggling her ass backward.

I swear she's trying to drive me mad. Standing in the water with her in my arms had been perfect, but Lauren ruined the moment. She's still too scared to give herself to me in any real capacity without her thinking there's a booby trap behind every corner.

I turn on the engine before gripping her around the waist. There's something nice about being in this position with her between my legs. Or so I think until she takes off like a bat out of hell. My grip tightens as we jump the first wave, and I wonder if I've made the biggest mistake ever by letting her be in charge of our destiny.

I understand why she squealed every time I went over a wave and crashed down on the ocean. Unlike her, I at least knew what the hell I was doing.

Lauren screams with excitement, and I can't help but smile behind her.

She's experiencing the high of gliding across the surface, skipping over waves with ease and nothing in front of her except for blue ocean. It's one of the only natural highs I can get without putting my life in peril.

"Oh my God, this is amazing!" She turns abruptly, sending water shooting out across the ocean surface like a torrential rain.

I want to tap out and get the hell off the back of this with her at the helm. Maybe I should've thought twice before I climbed on the back with her. I do own two Jet Skis, and it probably would've been wiser for her to learn on her own without me against her back.

Every time we smash down against the surface, my cock rubs just the right way along her back. I can't stop the hard-on as I watch her breasts bounce uncontrollably. I can't take my eyes off them as her nipple almost pops out of the side, showing me just enough to give me complete wood.

"Take me to the dock so I can get one too!" I yell in her ear, trying to get her to hear over the roar of the engine.

She glances back, not watching where she's going and hits a wave the wrong way. We splash down into the water as the Jet Ski skids a few feet before finally dying.

I turn a few times in the water and find my way to the surface, choking on the water I hadn't expected to fill my mouth. "Are you okay?" I ask as soon as her head breaks through the surface.

"Holy shit. That was scary." Her eyes are wide, and she, too, chokes on the mouthful of water I'm sure she swallowed as we went under.

"Are you okay?" I ask again, suddenly panicked that she could've hurt herself from hitting the water as quickly as we did.

She starts to laugh through her coughing. "I'm fine. Shaking a little, but fine."

I swim to her and wrap my arm around her waist. "Maybe we should go in for a while."

She wipes away the water trickling into her eyes. "Why?"

"I don't want you to get hurt."

"I'm not that breakable, Antonio."

"I know." I feel like an asshole insinuating she's breakable. I didn't mean it that way. The entire weekend would be a bust if either one of us were to get injured.

She peers up at me, one eye closed to shield it from the sun. "You were right, though."

I pull her closer, rubbing her wet breasts into my pecs. "About?"

"That was the most damn fun I've had in a long time."

"The weekend's just starting, love. I promise you'll fall in love with the island before we leave. You'll be begging me to bring you back here."

With those words, she pushes away from me and starts to swim toward the shore. Damn it. Me and my big mouth. She's so damn skittish, like a feral cat trying to escape capture.

I grab the Jet Ski, pulling it with me as I swim after her and toward the sand. She's over twenty feet ahead of me, and there's no way I'll catch up to her. I'll have to wait until we're both on land to talk with her. Things need to be settled before this shit gets out of whack and the rest of the weekend becomes as dark as the impending afternoon storm that's rumbling in the distance.

■ ■ ■ ■ ■ ■ ■ ■

There's an uncomfortable silence as we finish the lunch I'd prepped for us before we headed out for a morning in the sun. Lauren's closed herself off and put up every wall possible to keep me at a distance. Any headway I'd made earlier has vanished, but I have to find a way back. I refuse to let the rest of our time together to be like this. Silent. Cold. I want the fun, free woman who was in front of me less than an hour ago.

I push my plate to the side and lean forward, placing my hands on the table. "Are we going to talk about this?"

She dabs the corner of her mouth with the crisp linen napkin before finally looking at me. "I don't know what this is." She nervously fingers the unused knife on the table.

"Us, Lauren."

"There's no us, Antonio."

We stare each other down.

I refuse to let the topic go. I don't care if I have to break down her walls one by one. If need be, I'll revert back to the terms of the contract and win her over by using her body against her.

I tap my fingertips against the tabletop, and she leans back in her chair, folding her arms in front of her. I raise an eyebrow, and she does the same, mocking me like a child.

"Up," I command as my willingness to play nice slips.

She scrunches her nose and peers up at me as I stand. "Why?"

I hover over her and place my face closer to hers. "You signed a contract, and since you don't seem to be enjoying me doing everything the civilized way, I'm calling in the terms."

She shoots out of her chair, causing it to fall backward and bounce off the wooden floor. "I am enjoying this." Her arms flail around wildly. "You're fucking with my head, Antonio. It's not fucking fair." She slams her palms against my chest with so much force, she almost knocks me backward.

I grab her wrists and hold her in place. "I'm not trying to fuck with your head."

She tries to pull away, but my hold is too strong. "Let me go."

She's like a bratty kid, and all I want to do is paddle her ass. "Not until we talk."

She snarls and glares at me. "Why are you such a prick?"

"You haven't seen that side of me, but you're getting pretty damn close," I growl. I never denied that I was an asshole, but I've been nothing but a gentleman since we stepped foot on this island. "I don't have time for the games you're playing."

She stops struggling, but she doesn't give in. "Games? You're the one playing games."

I pull her forward by her wrist, crushing my lips down on hers. I steal any words she's ready to spew my way before she has the chance. I dip my tongue inside her mouth, and her tongue dances with mine. The stiffness in her arm softens. There's no denying the chemistry we have when our bodies are locked together in a poetic dance like this.

She snakes her arm around my shoulders, and her fingernails dig into my skin. Releasing her arm, I slide my hands down her ass and lift her in the air, pressing her against me. I'm rock hard and ready to fuck her brains out—and maybe some sense into her as I do it.

I deepen the kiss. The only sounds in the room are our ragged breaths, the waves crashing in the distance, and the cracks of thunder as a storm nears. My fingers curl around her ass cheeks, squeezing them roughly.

"Say you don't want me," I murmur against her lips. "Say you don't want this." I taunt her.

Her eyes pop open and flash with anger. "Just shut up and fuck me."

I thought she'd never ask. Reaching down, I swipe my arm across the table and push everything onto the floor. Dishes break as they hit the hardwood and scatter. I rip her bikini bottom off as soon as her ass rests against the table. She gasps, sucking the air from my lungs as I toss them to the floor near the wreckage.

I'm not wasting another moment or giving her a chance to change her mind. I push her body down against the table and spread her legs. She flattens her back and watches me down the length of her body. Leaning forward, I seal my lips around her clit, sucking lightly to hear her whimper.

Pushing her legs farther apart, I flatten my tongue against her and circle her clit with just the right amount of pressure. Her bottom jolts off the table before her legs spread wider, wanting more. I push two fingers inside and her pussy constricts around me as if trying to pull them deeper.

She's moaning, writhing on the tabletop as I bring her close to orgasm. Her body's trembling and her legs are flexing with each swipe over her clit and thrust inside her beautiful, sweet cunt.

"Oh God," she calls out.

I smile against her skin and pull away. Before she has a chance to protest, I push my cock inside of her in one forceful thrust. I place my hands on her shoulders as she digs her heels into my ass. I'm not letting her body get away as I pound into her with so much force the table is screeching against the floor.

"Who's fucking you, Lauren?" I say through gritted teeth as our bodies collide.

"Antonio," she moans, and her eyes sear into me.

I lift her up and flip her over so she's on her stomach and barely able to stand on her tiptoes as I push her down against the table. "Whose pussy is this?"

She thrusts back into me. "Antonio's."

I smile to myself as I pound into her. Relentlessly, I chase the orgasm that's just within reach. Grabbing her hair in my palm, I pull her head back just enough to see her face. "Who owns you?"

The anger's back, and she doesn't speak at first. But when my thrusting stops, her mouth starts moving. "You do."

Satisfied with her answer and the way her pussy's chasing my cock, I pick up the pace and pound into her until my legs begin to burn and the orgasm climbs up my back. Reaching around her bottom, I press my fingers against her clit and give it a light squeeze. Within seconds, she's following me over the cliff to ecstasy.

Chapter 16

Lauren

"Dinner's ready."

I splash more water across my knees and wish I could stay in here forever. "Coming," I tell him and sigh.

I've been in the bathroom for more than hour, soaking my bruises from the roughness earlier. Antonio pushed my buttons and pissed me off. Not because what he said was a lie, but because he spoke so much truth that it scared the shit out of me.

I do want him. I do like him. More than I want to, but I'm not ready to give in so easily. Every second that passes puts us one step closer to reality where there's no us that could ever be possible.

I know I can't stay in here forever. Standing for a

moment, I lean forward and take a few deep breaths. How did I get myself into this mess?

You had a one-night stand with your archrival. Only I would have such luck to sleep with my literal enemy. I have to face him, and I can't hide behind my anger anymore. He sees right through me, and my body can't take another angry fuck.

After I towel myself off and slip on a sundress I'd picked out from the dozens of them that filled the closet, I walk toward the beach. The hazy glow of candles beckons me forward as I pad through the darkness toward the water.

Antonio's standing near a cloth-covered table, holding out a chair for me. "Feel better?"

I smile weakly. "Yes," I say as I slide into the chair.

He places his hand on my shoulder, and I glance up at him. He's smiling, almost relieved by my answer. The bath was divine, but I don't feel better. My emotions are more mixed up than they were this morning.

In less than twenty-four hours, we'll be back in the city, and all of this will just be a memory. How can my mind justify letting my heart become attached to this man who's been nothing but kind to me?

My insides are in a constant battle, and just when I think sanity has won, Antonio throws another wrench into the mix and makes everything come to a grinding halt.

He settles in the seat across from me, and although I want to focus solely on him, I can't help but take in his lavish dinner setting. While I relaxed in the tub, he had to run around to set everything up as perfectly as he did.

Buried in the sand are a dozen large, metal candelabras illuminating the table with a soft glow. The small round table sits off to the side of the blanket, the same one we'd fallen asleep on last night. It's covered with a white linen tablecloth and has two place settings with the most ornate yet modern china I've ever seen. New York strip, asparagus, and fingerling potatoes are perfectly prepared and piping hot.

"I hope you like everything." He smiles and gazes at me across the table.

"It's beautiful," I say as I drape the napkin across my lap and try not to tear up just a little bit at the beauty of this moment.

No man has ever prepared a meal for me or planned an entire weekend away where I'm to do nothing but enjoy myself. Antonio hasn't even asked me to help carry a dish. He's spared no expense and gone to so much trouble because he's trying to...I don't know. Is he courting me? Trying to make me his? Possibly. I still don't entirely buy that he wants to win me over. There's no possible way we can ride off into the sunset, dragging cans behind his Ferrari with a "Just Married" sign taped to the back window.

"A toast," he says, popping the bottle of already chilled champagne.

I hold my glass as he fills it, and I wait for him to pour himself a glass before I lift it from the table. I watch him closely and take in the shadows that cross over his rugged features in the relative darkness. He's absolutely stunning. Just as beautiful in his crisp ivory linen shirt and tan beach pants as he is with water rivulets dripping off his naked body.

"To the now," he says as he clinks his glass to mine.

I'm barely paying attention, daydreaming about his wet flesh under the morning sun from earlier today. "To the now," I repeat, finally coming back to a reality that doesn't involve nudity.

"Dig in," he says.

I cut my steak, breaking it down into tiny pieces and pushing the fatty bits to the side. "You shouldn't have gone to all this trouble."

"It was nothing."

I gaze across the table and smile genuinely for the first time in hours. "It's a lot of work. I don't know why you're being so good to me. You could've very easily told me to fuck off."

"Fuck off where?" He waves his knife and fork around the table. "There's nowhere for you to go."

"Fine. You could've thrown the steak on a paper plate and had me eat over the sink."

He blinks at me with his mouth hanging open in shock. "Who would do such a thing?"

I laugh softly at first, but the look on his face is so priceless that it grows into a full-on giggle.

Trent would do that. Hell, he did. The man didn't know a pot from a casserole dish, and I was lucky if he boiled me a slimy hotdog on a bun when starvation would set in. After a day of on and off fighting, he most certainly would've never prepared a romantic dinner on the beach under the stars.

"A lot of men, Antonio. A lot of men."

"Those aren't men. No real man would ever treat a woman that way."

I've heard Italian men are romantic, and Antonio is no different. He's over the top, and I'm not used to such thoughtfulness being put into every detail like he has done.

"Stick with me, love, and this will seem like a weak attempt to win your affection."

I don't even balk anymore when he calls me love. It's beautifully charming and sexy as hell with his accent. "We need to talk about what's going to happen when we return."

He stops eating and places his forearms against the edge of the table. "There's nothing to discuss."

"Tomorrow when we return to our lives, do we pretend this never happened and pick up right where we left off?"

"Back there," he says, motioning toward the ocean with his chin. "That's the pretend and not real life. The only thing that's real is right here, right now. Work is what we do, not who we are."

I ponder his words as I take a sip of champagne. I wish it were all that easy. Work is who we are. It's the very core of my being. I'm nothing without my work and the dream I've been chasing since I was a little girl.

"You make everything sound simple, but when we're back in Chicago, nothing will ever be this easy again," I reply, running my fingers up and down the water that's trickling down the sides of the champagne flute.

"We can come back next week." He grins. "My island is yours whenever you want to join me."

I shake my head and exhale. The fairy tale is nice, but if word got around that I am traipsing all over the globe with the competition, I'd lose my position along with my credibility. "Let's not kid ourselves, Antonio. You have a dick."

"A very large dick," he interrupts with a sly grin and a wink.

"You have a nice dick." I smile, but I won't throw him the compliment he wants so badly. "It affords you many indulgences that I'm not allowed as a woman."

"That's not true," he argues, but he's completely wrong.

"If word got out that I slept with you, I'd immediately be labeled a whore, and people would say that I tried to use my sexuality to win."

"Do people really still say bullshit like that? I'd say it was true of the business world twenty years ago, but not today. We've evolved as a society."

"Sadly, we haven't. Colleagues would pat you on the back for fucking me, but I'd be forced out of my company with a moderately sized severance package and nothing more."

He relaxes back into his chair, still holding the silverware in his hands, his arms on the edge of the table. "I'd never tell a soul, Lauren. You must believe this."

I reach for the champagne, needing more liquid courage to get through everything that will happen tonight. Not that I don't want to make love with him under the stars, but I don't want to risk shedding tears about it being the last time I ever experience something like this.

Antonio beats me to the bottle, gently pushing my hands away with a smile. "Let me."

"I don't think you'd ruin me intentionally. You've already had that chance. But people talk, and rumors start. Eventually, the story spins out of control, and we can't dictate the narrative. I can't risk this turning into something more than it is. I've enjoyed my time with you, Antonio, more than I want to admit. But we can't have anything more than this weekend."

He eyes me across the table as he fills my glass. "To the now, Lauren. To the now," he reminds me.

We're living in the moment and forgetting that reality will slam us square in the face with the biggest bitch slap I've probably ever experienced.

"To the now," I repeat, trying to convince myself and failing miserably.

Antonio

We're side by side on the blanket, our fingers laced together and our shoulders touching as we stare up at the sky.

"What's your favorite planet?" she asks.

A moment ago, she was telling me about her time spent in Boston and how their Little Italy rivals even Chicago's and now she's talking about the tiny pinpoints of light above us.

"Jupiter."

She turns her head toward me, the moonlight shimmering across her dew-kissed skin. "Why Jupiter?"

"There's an understated beauty to the planet. From afar, it looks serene, almost like a giant topaz turning against the darkness. But beneath the cloud, there's nothing peaceful. The storm under the beautiful clouds has raged for millions of years and has never diminished over time."

She faces the sky again, staring at the moon shining directly overhead. "That's an interesting choice. Mine's Saturn," she says, tightening her grasp on my fingers.

"Everyone loves Saturn, Lauren."

"Wouldn't it be amazing to go there someday? Can you imagine the view of the rings intertwined with the fifty-three moons passing by the night sky each night? It must be breathtaking."

"Someday, sooner than we both can even imagine, humans will land on Saturn, and we'll finally get our first glimpse at the night sky. I'll keep my feet firmly planted here and marvel at the photos."

"Maybe the future will be like Star Trek, and we can just beam ourselves anywhere in the universe."

"Can you get your team on that? They seem to be able to make the impossible a reality." I smile at her, but she doesn't smile back. I roll onto my side, placing one arm above her head and draping the other across her stomach. "Thank you," I whisper.

"For what?" She finally smiles.

"For making me happy this weekend."

She lifts her hand, pressing her palm against my cheek. "It's you who's made me happy, Antonio. I can't remember the last time I've felt this free."

"You deserve this and more, love. Never doubt the value of freedom and remembering what life is truly about."

"I haven't found the balance yet."

"Stay with me, and I'll show you how to have everything you've ever dreamed."

Her thumb brushes against my lips. "You say such pretty and fanciful things."

I lean forward, dragging my lips across hers. "It's not fanciful if I can make it a reality. I would move mountains to have this time with you again."

"Even if it meant giving up Interstellar?" She raises an eyebrow, her hand still against my cheek.

"I'd give up my world to be with you, Lauren."

She lifts her head and presses her lips to mine. I cradle her neck in my hand and kiss her back, deep and demanding.

I want her to feel the truth in my words.

I'd move heaven and earth if I believed Lauren could be mine forever.

Lifting my body, I gently put my weight on her as I climb between her legs. If there's a heaven, this would be it. Our bodies tangled together, our lips joined, and our hearts beating wildly out of control with everything else in the world unimportant.

Unlike earlier today, there's no anger in our actions. I want to take her slow and make love to her, expressing everything that's bottled up inside through my touch.

When I finally slide into her, our eyes are locked. I gaze down at her as she peers up at me. There's no uncertainty or hesitation in our movements. Just a slow, steady rhythm as I rock into her and she pushes back, needy and wanting more.

The orgasm makes my toes curl and my head spin as my heart beats out of rhythm, and I gasp for air.

Collapsing onto my back, I pull her flush against me. "Let's stay here forever."

She laughs softly. "We have to go back, Antonio."

"We don't. We have enough money to live the rest of our lives right here and never face reality again."

She runs the edge of her fingernail up the middle of my pecs. "Although I love the sound of that, we have people in our lives who matter. I can't run away, not yet, at least."

I drift to sleep with Lauren in my arms and a head swimming with possibilities.

Chapter 17

Lauren

My sundress blows in the ocean breeze as I stand near the edge, letting the water crash over my bare feet. I dig my toes into the sand, memorizing every inch of the island and the way the wind kisses my skin with each pass.

I'm not ready to give this up. The last two days have made me realize that I haven't been enjoying my life to the fullest. With the early death of my parents, I know that life can be fleeting and that I shouldn't take time for granted.

There isn't an infiniteness to life. Not even the universe will be around forever. It's rapidly expanding until someday it'll all end in something more spectacular than the Big Bang. Interstellar is still my baby, but I know I have to slow down and take time out for me. One day I don't want to look back and realize I missed out on the beauty of life, stuck in an office, with nothing to show for it but a few awards and a bank account full of money.

Being with Antonio has been easier than I ever imagined. There's an easiness to us. He's someone I could share my life with if it weren't for the complication of our companies being at odds. He's the type of man I could share my fears and achievements with, instead of holding them all inside and trying to do everything alone.

Even though a relationship between us would be impossible, he's made me want someone at my side to share everything with. My heart's heavy because I know when we step foot off this island, nothing will ever be the same.

I reach down, picking up a perfect seashell near my feet and clutching it tightly in my palm. It's the single reminder of this weekend and Antonio that I'll allow myself to bring back home. I can't wallow in self-pity, wishing life could be different. We both must play the cards we're dealt, even if they put thousands of miles between us.

We spent most of the day on the beach, talking and swimming under the warm Caribbean sun. I didn't think about the contract I'd signed or the fact that everything was coming to an end. I saved that until now, until the end of this journey with Antonio.

His arm wraps around my shoulders, and his toes meet the crashing waves. "Are you ready to go back?"

I place my head against his chest and stare off into the distant blackness. "I know we have to, but my heart doesn't want to leave here, Antonio."

"We can come back," he says quickly. His hand curls around my shoulder, pulling me closer. "This doesn't have to be the end."

He's uttered that phrase to me a dozen times this weekend, but he's wrong. This does have to end. There's no us on the mainland. There's no reality where two rivals can fall madly in love and have a happily ever after. It's delusional even to let my mind wander there.

"Thank you," I say, peering into his blue eyes that are as dark as the ocean in the dim lighting.

"Thank you, love." His fingers touch my chin, lifting my lips to his.

I'm almost breathless as he kisses me. The wind swirls around us as the waves crash down against our feet. If I could have a single photograph from this weekend, this moment would be it. When his lips leave mine, he stares down at me with the same sadness in his eyes I have in my heart.

Neither of us wants this moment to end, but we both know it must. The dreamland we've lived since Friday night is just that...a dream and can never be reality.

"The jet's ready."

I try to crack a smile, but I fail miserably. "I'm ready," I lie and slide my arm around his back.

I glance at the sea, taking in the whitecaps of the waves that are illuminated by the moonlight cascading across the sea. The tranquility yet volatility brewing under the surface is much like this moment. Perfectly peaceful, yet filled with dread and fear that I'll never be the same again.

Antonio and I walk to the dock and the waiting charter to take us to the mainland, our arms around each other and our sides touching. After Antonio helps me inside the tiny boat, I take one last glance at the lights dotting the wraparound patio, the palm trees waving in the wind, and I say a final goodbye.

Not even the most beautiful things in life are meant to last. This is another step on my journey and one I'll never forget.

Antonio

"Welcome home, Mr. Forte," the airport hangar manager says as we step out of the jet into the cool Chicago air. "Your car is ready for you."

Lauren's already halfway down the stairs, heading toward the waiting Escalade before I have a chance to respond to the manager.

I give him a curt nod before jogging down the stairs, reaching for Lauren's hand. "Wait," I say, but she pulls away and doesn't look back.

She stalks toward the opposite side of the car and slides into the back seat before I can even open the door for her. The Lauren Bradley of last week is back and in full effect.

After I climb in the back and give her address to the driver, I take a moment to think about what to say next.

She's pissed at me and rightfully so. I promised her the name of the mole, and I've been vague with my answer. She wants specifics, but I'm not ready to lose the only card I have left.

"I expect the name by tomorrow or..." Her voice trails off.

"Tomorrow you'll have your mole," I promise, and now I have to deliver.

I pull a manila folder that's been tucked in the pocket behind the passenger seat that I had prepared for this moment, hoping the weekend would go as planned. "I have another proposition for you."

"Oh, another?" She purses her lips and glares at me. "Is this another thing you won't fully deliver on too?"

I deserved that shitty comment. "I will deliver, Ms. Bradley. This is entirely different than our personal agreement. This involves both of our companies."

She turns toward me, pressing her back against the door and putting as much distance between us as possible. Her eyes glance down at the folder. "At this moment, I can't trust anything you have to say or any contract you have to offer."

I straighten my back and let her words go. The last thing I want to do is argue with her. "Look this over, and we'll discuss it in the morning."

Her top lip curls as she glares at me. "Just tell me what's inside. I don't have time to read through a hundred-page contract. I have a company to run, Mr. Forte."

"Cozza is ready to move forward with the takeover of Interstellar. Nothing has changed, and no matter how hard I try, I can't get the board to change their minds."

Her eyes narrow. "Like you've bothered to sway them in any way. This was all just a ruse to get me away while the takeover moved forward. Just admit it."

That's the furthest thing from the truth, but she'll never believe me. "Inside this folder is a new contract, an agreement to bring to your board and investors. Instead of a hostile takeover, Cozza would like to merge with Interstellar to create a new company that no one could top."

"So, wait." She gawks at me. "You want us to join up and make a team?"

"Imagine our two companies with us in charge and the amazing and unbelievable things we could accomplish together. Number one and number two joining forces would make us unstoppable. The aerospace industry would grow by leaps and bound through cooperation instead of competition."

"You're delusional," she replies and closes her eyes. "My team will never go for this, nor will my investors."

"Read the document, Lauren. Don't make a rash decision before understanding the true terms and what Cozza has to offer. This could make your investors richer than they've ever imagined and make a trip to Saturn a reality sooner than we both expect. We'd be unstoppable."

She rips the folder from my hands and sets it in her lap, maintaining her distance from me. "When do you want an answer?"

"Tomorrow, end of business. I'll deliver you the identity of the mole, and you give me an answer if you're willing to bring this option in front of your board."

"Do I have a choice but to bring it before them? It's not my decision to make."

"But it would be your decision if you'd like to remain at the company and work with me."

Her eyes rake up and down my body with disgust. "I will not be your second-in-command."

"You'd become the President of Cozza Interstellar Corp, and I'd maintain my position as CEO. You would not be my underling, but my equal."

"It would never work."

"Lauren," I say, reaching across the seat and placing my hand on her knee, but her body remains rigid. "Just think about it. This could solve all of our problems. No longer would we be enemies and have to maintain a safe distance. We could be equal partners and become something bigger and more profound."

She doesn't reply as she straightens her body to face forward, causing my hand to slip off her knee. The wall that had crumbled is back up and stronger than ever. I fear it's impenetrable at this point and there's nothing I can do to remove even a single brick from her self-imposed armor.

She stares out the window as the car weaves in and out of the city traffic. The only thing I can do is hope that once she reads over the contract, she'll come back to me.

I've always been the master of my own destiny. But this time, I'm leaving it in her hands. I've played my cards, dealt every last one in this final hand, and the decision rests with her, along with our fate. For once, I'm giving in and letting her make the decision that will determine our futures.

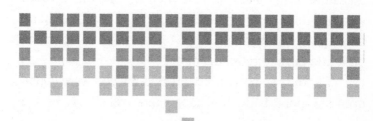

Chapter 18

Lauren

There are exactly eleven voice mails and seventeen text messages from Tara when I finally turn on my phone after I cracked open a bottle of Moscato and kicked off my shoes.

Tara: Want to get a drink tonight?

Tara: Hello.

Tara: Are you wrapped up in that handsome devil?

Tara: Lauren, where the fuck are you?

Tara: I'm going to call the police.

Tara: Damn it, why didn't you tell me you were going out of town? I called Cassie to see if she knew where your ass was. Call me as soon as you get in.

I listen to the voice mails as I sip the first glass. They're funny at first before growing panicked and then telling my ass off just like she had in the text messages. I'm about to dial her number when there's a pounding at the door.

I stare at it, not moving because it's after ten and the doorman hasn't alerted me to a guest. The only person who has unfettered access to my loft is Tara. I could sit here quietly and pretend not to be home or open the door and have to retell the entire story.

"I know you're home. Matt told me you were. Open up." She pounds on the door again, relentless as she always is.

I'll be having a chat with Matt, the doorman, tomorrow about the type of information he shares, even with my best friend. I open the door and don't say a word as Tara breezes into my place and tosses her purse to the floor.

"Where the hell have you been?" she asks, plopping down on my plush, oversized couch and making herself comfortable. "You have a tan."

I grab a second glass from the cabinet next to the sink, along with another bottle of wine because I don't feel like sharing. I need to drown my sorrows and any thoughts I may be having in lots of booze. "I went to the Caribbean for the weekend."

"Which island?" She plucks the glass from my hand before my butt touches the cushion. "You know I love it there."

"I don't think it had a name. It was a private island."

Her mouth drops open as she pours herself a glass of wine and tops mine off. "Wait. Were you with him?"

I nod and let out a loud sigh. She stares at me, wanting details. I can see it in her eyes, but I gulp down the glass and reach for the bottle again.

She's quicker and moves it out of reach, holding it hostage. "Were you with him?"

"Yes, I was with him. Now give me the wine." I motion for the bottle and can't bear to look her in the eye.

She tucks her leg under her bottom and rubs her hands together. "If you're ready to take him down, I've come up with a plan. But first, I want to know everything that happened."

And with that, I tell her. I go into every detail. I leave nothing out. I tell her about our first night under the stars and sleeping by the sea in his arms. I recount our fights and that I finally rode a Jet Ski after she's been begging me to for years. I relive the candlelight dinner on the beach. Tara sits silent, hanging on every word as I speak.

"God, he sounds dreamy."

"Like a frickin' nightmare," I mutter and take another gulp of wine.

I'm three glasses in and not feeling half bad. The wine's dulled the ache that's settled deep in my stomach since the moment the jet touched down. The pain of saying goodbye to Antonio and knowing that nothing will ever be the same. The wine has even tamped down the anger I have for him and the rage that's built inside since the moment he refused to tell me the identity of the mole.

"Come on." She slaps my arm and rolls her eyes. "I'd take a little of your nightmare. I mean, shit," she mumbles. "You could've worked my shifts for me, and I could've lounged on the beach and made love to that beautiful man. I'm willing to take one for the team."

"The nightmare wasn't the weekend. The nightmare has only just begun, Tara."

She grimaces. "What are you going to do?"

I scrub my hand across my face and try to focus my blurry, tired eyes. "I have no idea."

"Could what he's proposing work?"

"I guess it could."

I haven't put a lot of thought into it. He dumped all the information in my lap, and I haven't had time to process the full scope of the proposal. I'm too angry with him to even see straight, let alone form a coherent thought.

"I say go for it. You get the man, the company, and can rule the world."

I laugh because she always makes everything seem so simple. "If only it were that easy."

"It is. Then you can take me to that swanky private island, and we can bask in the sun and work on our tans."

"I'll buy my own private island just for us."

She scoots forward and places her empty glass on the coffee table. "Now you're talking, sister, but maybe hire a really hot cabana boy for us to ogle."

I laugh. "I can do that."

She glances down at her watch before climbing to her feet. "I have to go. It's late, and I know you're going to be in the office before the sun even rises."

I walk her to the door, sad to have my friend leave so quickly. "Thanks for checking on me, T."

She wraps her arms around me and holds me tight. "Just promise to call me tomorrow and let me know what happens."

"I promise. You'll be the first to know what I tell Antonio."

"How about an early dinner tomorrow to celebrate?"

"Celebrate?" I ask as we pull away from each other.

"Whatever your decision is, I know it'll be right. I could use a fabulous meal and more wine, or we can grab a bat and visit Mr. Forte." She laughs, and although she's joking, I know she'd break his knees in a heartbeat. "I'll swing by your office at five, and we can have a girls' night."

By the time tomorrow evening rolls around, I'm going to need time with my friend. I don't know if I'll be in tears or ready to take the world by storm. "You got a deal."

Tara waves as she strides toward the elevator, pretending to punch the air like she's preparing for a fight. She's the female version of Rocky minus the heavyweight titles and muscles. But the girl has the attitude of a fighter and has always been by my side, no matter what crazy shit's gone down in my life.

I close the door and press my back against the cool, hard wood, taking in my expansive penthouse before sliding to the floor. Resting my head in my hands, I groan.

"I fucked it all up, Daddy," I say, wishing he were here more than anyone in the world. "I think I did it this time."

The only person I can turn to now is Tara, and she wasn't much help. Dangle a sexy man in front of her, and she's choosing that option, no matter the repercussions. She doesn't see the downside, no matter how small it may be.

When I'm done having my pity party, I make it to my bed before passing out fully dressed and completely exhausted.

Not only did traveling take its toll on me, but the emotional turmoil that's coursing through me has drained every ounce of energy I had left in my system. I dream of Antonio, haunting me from the beach and beckoning for me to join him by the ocean under our stars.

■ ■ ■ ■ ■ ■ ■ ■

"We may have found something," Josh says before I've even had a chance to shove my purse in my desk drawer. "It's not much, but it may be a lifeline."

Cassie saunters in, eyeing Josh, who isn't always her favorite person. "I brought you a cup of coffee, Ms. Bradley. Is there anything else I can get you?"

Josh is staring at me as I take the coffee from Cassie's hands. "That'll be all, Cassie." I smile at her before my eyes flicker to Josh.

I wait for Cassie to close the door as she leaves before I speak, but Josh interrupts me first. "Looks like you had a relaxing weekend."

I glance down at my tan skin and drag my eyes back to his. "I spent the weekend trying to save our company. There's another offer on the table from Cozza."

Josh places his hands together, touching his fingers to his chin. "What type of offer?"

"They're offering a merger instead of a takeover."

He leans back, placing his ankle on his opposite knee, and he stares at me with an unreadable expression.

"As the CEO, I'm bound to bring the offer before the board for a vote, but I have reservations."

His fingertips slide over his jawline in slow, gentle strokes. "Do you want me to look it over?"

I reach into my purse and pull out the manila folder before sliding it across the table. "Everything's in here. Let me know your thoughts."

"It's a total merger instead of a takeover. Would we remain on staff?"

"We would," I tell him, based on everything I read this morning on my way to work. "The name would change and our roles may end up being slightly different, but we'd become Cozza Interstellar Corp or CIC and become the largest and most powerful aerospace company in the world."

He flips the folder open and studies the first page. "Based on what the team brought me over the weekend, it may be our only option."

"We'll meet after lunch to discuss the logistics and what the offer could mean for the future of this company."

He stands, tapping the folder against his open palm. "I'll give you my opinion then, but I really don't see another way out of this without ripping our company apart."

"I was afraid of that," I tell him before he walks out of my office.

I figured a company such as Cozza wouldn't put a takeover in motion unless they were completely sure they'd be successful. I'm sure their team of lawyers and executives worked every angle.

Even though the takeover would be costly with the new engine ready to go into production, they'd more than make the money back. There isn't much risk on their end, and the merger is a lifeline that I'm sure Antonio put into motion.

The offer may be the only way I get to keep some form of the company I've worked my ass off to propel to greatness, without turning into the fall guy and sacrificial lamb.

Chapter 19

Lauren

"It's a go, Lauren. The offer is really solid." Josh tosses the folder onto my desk and stares down at me. "It's the only way I can see that we can save everything we've worked so hard for over the last few years."

I rub the back of my neck because I never wanted to be in this situation in the first place. "I'll set a board meeting before we open it up for shareholding voting. The final decision will have to be approved by a majority."

"They'll approve it because they're ruled by money. Not everyone has given their life to this company like we have. Some people just care about the bottom line."

I smile weakly and know he's right. "I'll have Cassie schedule it after I speak with Mr. Forte and his team this afternoon."

"Do you want me there as backup?"

I laugh softly at his kind gesture, but I've never needed backup before. "I'll handle the people at Cozza. If you can start preparing a report to present to the board, that would be a huge help."

"I'm on it," he says as he walks toward the door. "Maybe I'll finally be able to get some sleep tonight."

"I think we all will, Josh."

He smiles back at me before leaving, and guilt floods me. My entire team spent the weekend stressing out and trying to find a way to save the company, while I lay on the beach and fell in love with the enemy.

Trent: Can you come to the test hangar? There's an issue.

The text message from Trent has me out of my office, clutching my phone, and headed toward the parking garage within seconds.

Any issue with the engine could not only end the terms of the new deal, but it could bring down the value of Interstellar so dramatically that we'd be prime pickings for a takeover and not a merger.

My hands are shaking as I weave through city traffic and the knot in my gut tightens as the hangar comes into view. I can't believe there's an issue with the engine this many days out from the success and very public unveiling.

My heels click against the painted cement floor as I walk through the empty hangar toward Trent's office. The wind blows, causing goose bumps to break out across my skin, and I long for the warm ocean breezes of the Caribbean and the ease of life on a remote and desolate island.

"What's the issue?" I ask as soon as the door swings open.

Trent's sitting behind his desk with his face hidden by the computer screen. "One second," he says casually.

I squeeze my phone so tightly, I'm surprised the screen doesn't shatter into a million pieces. "I rush over here, and now you think I'm going to wait?"

"Calm down, Lulu. I just need a second." His tongue darts out and sweeps across his lip as he presses a few more buttons on the keyboard. "Sit down for a minute and relax."

"Relax?" I hover over his desk and glare down at him. "You said there's an issue, and you expect me to relax?"

If I wouldn't get fired and be arrested, I'd launch myself over the desk and wrap my hands around his wide neck and choke the life right out of him.

He pushes back from his desk, switching off the monitor before standing. "Let me show you the problem," he says, motioning toward the hangar with his head.

"I don't have time for bullshit. Let's get to it because I have a company to run." I'm seething with anger, and his carefree attitude is pushing me over the edge as I follow him.

"It's around back," he says, motioning for me to follow as I keep a safe distance from him so I don't wind up in handcuffs. "You look good, Lulu. Different."

I growl as his eyes flicker up and down my body, ogling me in a way that makes my skin crawl. I give him a shitty smile and stop walking. "Where are you taking me?"

He stops and turns to face me, his eyes still raking over me. "I forgot the papers in my car. We're going to grab them."

I grit my teeth together so hard they squeak. "Why didn't you bring them in here while I drove over here?"

"I was busy getting work done. I have to keep the boss happy."

I ball my fists at my sides and walk past him, heading toward the same spot he's parked his car for the last half a dozen years. "Let's make this quick, and it better be good."

He jogs to catch up to me as I take long strides across the parking lot. "It'll be good. I promise." He smiles smugly.

I stand to the side, leaning against his Tahoe as he opens the back. He reaches inside and pulls out a folder of paperwork and spreads it across the inside. "Look at this," he says and points to the sheet right in the middle.

I can't make out the words from where I'm standing, and he backs away, knowing I'm angry. I walk in front of him and pick up the piece of paper, studying it.

It's nonsense. There's nothing of value on the paper in my hands. A jumble of emails sent between me and office staff. When I flip it over, I freeze. It's a word for word transcript of text messages between me and Forte.

"You've been a busy girl, Lulu." He clicks his tongue against the roof of his mouth, and his shadow covers me, sending a chill down my spine.

I spin on my heels and wave the piece of paper between us. "How did you get this?"

"I have my ways. I did so much for you," he says and places his hands on my arms, squeezing tighter than usual. "I did all of this for you, and this is how you repay me?"

I take a step back, trying to put space between us and free myself from his hold, but my ass knocks into the bumper, and I know I have nowhere else to go. "Get your hands off me, Trent."

"I told you you'd always be mine, Lulu."

I'm just about to scream when his hand covers my mouth.

"Shh, no one can hear you out here, and no one's coming to save you." His eyes are cold and distant as he peers down at me.

Alarm bells that were ringing faintly are now blaring so loudly I can't hear anything else except my own heartbeat as it thumps wildly in my chest.

"Are you going to play nice, or do I have to take you against your will?"

Take me? Where the fuck is he going to take me? "I'll play nice," I say against his hand, almost gagging on the taste of his skin against my tongue.

As soon as his hand eases up, I try to run, but he pulls me backward until I collide with his chest. I claw at his arms, trying to break free, but he's too strong. A hand wraps around my neck, squeezing so tightly that my face starts to prickle. "There's no getting away from me. You're mine always and forever."

I don't stop struggling. Not as the blackness starts to come and my eyes go blurry. I fight with everything I have because I refuse to go out like this. The man I once thought I loved is trying to kill me, and I'm powerless to stop him. He's too strong for me to fight off.

In my final moments of consciousness, there's only one person I think about... Antonio.

Antonio

"Where is she?" Tara, Lauren's friend from the restaurant, asks as soon as I walk inside Lauren's office for our scheduled meeting.

"I don't know. I was supposed to meet her right now." I glance down at my watch. I'm not late. One thing I know about Lauren is she's always on time.

"Something's not right," she says, chewing on her fingernail as she paces the carpet in front of Lauren's desk. "We were meeting for dinner. Cassie hasn't seen her in hours, but she went looking for her."

"Wait, what?" Panic seeps into my veins as her words set in. "How long has she been missing?"

"Three hours." Tara yanks at her hair with the most frightful look. "I thought maybe she was with you, pulling another disappearing act like this weekend."

Oh God. Dread seizes me. "She wasn't with me, and I haven't talked to her in hours."

Tara walks over to Lauren's desk and pulls out her purse. "She hasn't gone far. Her things are here, but no phone. I already called, but she didn't answer."

Cassie comes storming into the office. "Trent's gone too," she says, hunching over like she's been running.

"Who's Trent?"

"Her ex-boyfriend and the head researcher here."

I stumble back a step.

"He's been harassing her for months, but Lauren couldn't bring herself to fire him with the progress he'd made on Mercury."

All the pieces click together. Lauren's missing. Trent's MIA, and they have a checkered past.

"He never quite got over her," Cassie tells us.

"I'll shatter him into a million pieces," I say, trying to control the anger that's bubbling inside me. "If he hurts her, I'll end his life with my bare hands."

"Oh, fuck," Tara hisses, grasping at her chest as she eases herself into Lauren's chair.

"I'll find her. Don't tell anyone else she's missing until I can figure out where Trent is. If you tell the cops, I'll have to follow the law. I can work faster without the constraints of the legal system."

"I want to help," Tara says as she pops up from the chair.

"Tara." I grasp her by the shoulders as she comes to a stop in front of me. "I need you to go to her place and let me know if she shows up." Tara nods, but her eyes are filling with tears. "I promise I'll find her."

"What about me?" Cassie asks with an ashen face.

"Go home at your usual time and stow Lauren's purse. Lock her office, and if anyone asks, she's gone to Cozza for a last-minute meeting."

"Yes, sir." Cassie covers her face with her hands.

"I will bring her back, ladies. I'll move heaven and earth to bring Lauren back."

I don't care if I have to kill a thousand men, I will find her. Lord help the man who has her. He won't come out unscathed or die a quick, painless death.

Chapter 20

I lurch awake to the distant sound of metal striking metal. I jolt upright, curling my fingers around the base of my neck.

Trent was choking me.

I suck in a breath and cough when the air hits the back of my throat. The burning sensation is so intense, I hold my breath, trying to calm the ache.

He attacked me. Trent attacked me.

I blink a few times, trying to see through the darkness, but it's no use. There's not even a pinprick of light where I sit. I wave my hand in front of me, but I see nothing as my fingers pass by my face.

Where am I?

"Trent!" I yell, but it comes out garbled and hoarse.

There's no reply, and for a moment, I'm thankful.

Maybe I shouldn't have called for him. I thought I knew the man, but clearly, I don't understand the first thing about him. If he's willing to choke me until I black out and then kidnap me, God only knows what else he'll do.

He kidnapped me.

The realization settles in my bones, and I'm momentarily panicked.

Breathe, Lauren. You're a survivor.

At the moment, I am alive, and I plan to do everything in my power to keep it that way too.

Earlier, when I started to black out, I thought I'd never wake up again.

Fear had gripped me as he tightened his fingers around my throat, and I tried to fight him off. I scratched his skin, marking him as evidence in case.

In case of what?

I waited to see the light people seem to claim calls a soul as we die, but I saw nothing. I waited to see my father, almost welcoming him because I haven't felt whole since he died, but he never came. I was only greeted by the darkest black I'd ever known.

Pulling my knees under my chin, I wrap my arms around my legs and begin to rock back and forth. I swallow a few times, trying to calm the sting each time I breathe, but my mouth's too dry for it to work.

I rock forward, propelling myself to my feet and reach into the darkness.

I have to get out of here.

Wherever here may be.

My fingers press against a smooth, metal wall, and I flatten my palms as I feel my way up and down the surface in front of me. When I reach the corner, I step carefully and continue.

After making my way around the room, I start to panic when I realize there's no door or anything except the four walls surrounding me. I back away slowly, moving toward what I assume is the center of the room.

I don't want to die. Not like this. I figured I'd live to be old and feeble, forgetting who I was and dribbling my mashed potatoes down the front of my frilly shirt the nurses at the old-age home would dress me in. I never thought Trent had the ability to do this to me, but if he could choke me until I blacked out, how far is he from wrapping his fingers around my neck until I take my final breath?

I curl into a ball on the floor and let the sob hovering at the back of my throat break free. The echo inside the room is loud, and I cover my mouth with my hand to muffle the sound of my cries.

The sound of a latch opening, scraping against the metal as the bolt passes, makes me freeze. I hold my breath, not wanting the darkness to end.

I'm not ready to face the man who's trying to take everything from me. I hold my breath and lie perfectly still, pretending to be unconscious.

The door opens with a loud creak, but I still don't dare look. Heavy footsteps move closer and grow louder as he approaches.

I will not die.

I won't give in.

I have to fight.

To be continued...

Merger release November 28th.
Now available for preorder on all retailers.

chellebliss.com/takeover

Other Books by Chelle Bliss

~**MEN OF INKED SERIES**~
THROTTLE ME - Book 1
HOOK ME - Book 2
RESIST ME - Book 3
UNCOVER ME - Book 4
WITHOUT ME - Book 5
HONOR ME - Book 6
WORSHIP ME – Book 7

~**ALFA PI SERIES**~
SINFUL INTENT- Book 1
UNLAWFUL DESIRE - Book 2
WICKED IMPULSE - Book 3

~**STANDALONE BOOKS**~
REBOUND NOVELLA
ENSHRINE
TOP BOTTOM SWITCH
DIRTY WORK
DIRTY SECRET
UNTANGLE ME
KAYDEN THE PAST
MISADVENTURES OF A CITY GIRL

chellebliss.com/books

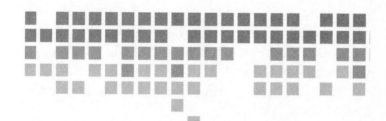

A letter to readers...

Dear Readers and Friends,

Don't get the pitchforks out yet. I know you're screaming right now, scaring your friends and family, but I swear the wait will be worth it.

Luckily, Merger releases in 4 weeks on November 28th so you don't have to wait for long. I've never written a cliffhanger before and this could very well blow up in my face, but I loved had a ball writing the start of their story.

I hope you'll take a moment and leave a review, but try and be nice. If you loved the story, don't take stars off because it was a cliffhanger. Does anyone leave bad reviews for a television show when they have to wait for the next episode or the next season? Gasp. We'd have no reason to watch the next one if everything is tied up in a pretty little bow.

I hope you'll pick up Merger and see how Antonio and Lauren's story ends. Remember, it releases November 28th everywhere.

If you're a new reader, I hope you'll take a moment and check out the other titles I have available. The list is long, so be ready to for a read-a-thon. There's an excerpt to Enshrine after the About the Author section. It's a heart-wrenching story but I promise you'll smile in the end.

If you're a long time reader... thank you for loving my books.

Feel free to each out to me anytime. I try to answer emails at least once a week. You can contact me at authorchellebliss@gmail.com

Thanks again for reading. Merger will be out before you know it.

Sincerely,
Chelle Bliss

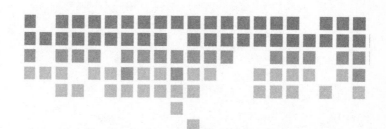

About the Author

Chelle Bliss is the USA Today bestselling author of the Men of Inked and ALFA P.I. series. She hails from the Midwest, but currently lives near the beach even though she hates sand. She's a full-time writer, time-waster extraordinaire, social media addict, coffee fiend, and ex high school history teacher. She loves spending time with her two cats, alpha boyfriend, and chatting with readers. To learn more about Chelle, please visit *chellebliss.com*.

Join Chelle's Newsletter
www.chellebliss.com/newsletter

Chelle's TEXT Alerts (US Only)
Text *BLISS* to 24587

chellebliss.com

Throttle Me

NOW AVAILABLE

Download the eBook for ***FREE*** at

chellebliss.com/inkedseries

"Ready, babe?" He motioned toward the door.

I wanted to scream no, but I didn't have a choice. I could never walk into this sort of place on my own.

"Yeah, ready as I'll ever be." I started walking toward the door and felt a hand on my arm, stopping me in my tracks. I looked at his fingers wrapped around my arm and turned toward him. "What are you doing?"

"You can't just walk into a place like this. You're an outsider. They'll eat you alive in there. I don't want anyone giving you shit. We have to make them believe you're with me so they leave you the fuck alone. Unless you want the attention?" he asked with a crooked eyebrow.

"I don't." I didn't mind the idea of making everyone in the bar think we were together. City was hot and seemed like a nice guy; he did stop to help me when he could've driven right by me.

"Just stay by my side and follow my lead. I know these people and I don't want them sniffing around you. They look for easy prey," he said, giving me a smile that made my body tingle and my sex convulse.

"Okay, I'll stick to you like glue and follow your lead." Jesus, I sounded like a dork. I've always been a bookworm. I was national honor society member, and when all my friends were partying, I stayed in my dorm to study.

City nestled me against his side, tucking me between his body and arm. I moved with him, trying to keep up with his fluid movements, but my legs were so short I felt like I almost had to jog to keep time with him. He opened the door and I was immediately hit with a smoky smell, loud, twangy music, and a dozen set of eyes looking directly at us.

Randomly people yelled out "City" throughout the bar, giving me a clue that he was a regular. I felt like I'd entered a seedy version of Cheers and City was Norm, only sexy and muscular. He leaned down, placing his mouth next to my ear. I felt his hot breath before I could hear his words.

"Stick close and show no fear," he whispered, causing goose bumps to break out across my skin. "Let's say hello then we'll call a tow for you."

City looked big enough to handle any man in this place, but I didn't want to take that chance. I concentrated on breathing, keeping my chin up, and watching where I walked. The floor was filled with peanut shells and dust, and it made the walk in the stilettos even more treacherous than normal. I could barely walk when I bought them, but they looked too sexy to pass up.

We walked to a table filled with men all wearing their leather vests, covered in patches. They were unshaven, as dangerously sexy as City, with mischievous smiles on their faces. "Who's this lovely lady, City?" one man asked. His eyes raked up my body, stopping at my breasts before he looked at my face.

"This is Sunshine. Don't even fucking think about it, Tank, she's with me," City said with a smile on his face as he pulled me closer.

Sunshine? I'd never told him my name and he never asked. I didn't like the way Tank looked at me. Thank God he wasn't the one driving by while I was stranded. He looked at me like I was a piece of meat, a meal for his enjoyment.

Tank put his hands up in surrender. "Dude, I'd never. Chill the fuck out. I'm just enjoying the view," he said, his eyes moving from City to me, and not being coy about his visual molestation.

City squeezed my waist. "Sunshine, this is Tank, the asshole. This is Hog, Frisco, and Bear," he said, pointing to each of the men.

The nicknames didn't seem to fit any of the men, except Bear. His arms were hairy and he was big, huge, in fact, with dark hair and a fuzzy face. He looked huggable and kind, with soft hazel eyes.

"Hi," I said, looking at each of them quickly, but I didn't try to memorize their names.

"I didn't know you were bringing a woman tonight, City," Bear said.

"Wilder shit has happened, Bear," City said, pulling me closer, leaving no space between us.

"She doesn't look like your usual taste, my friend." Bear smirked. "I don't mean that shitty, girl, I just mean you're one fine piece of ass and too good for that low-life motherfucker. You should be sitting on my lap." He patted his leg, and I wanted to find an exit. I looked down and studied my clothes. I didn't wear the trashy clothes some of the women in here wore, but I looked classy, sexy even, with not a hint of nerd to be found.

City moved toward Bear, and my heart sank as he began to speak. "Show some respect, you asshole. That's not how you talk to a lady." City stood inches from Bear's face. "Apologize to the lady. Now." City towered over him as Bear stayed rooted in his chair.

Bear looked at me, and I could see him swallow hard before he spoke. "I'm sorry, Sunshine. I was just kidding around. I really am an asshole. Forgive me, please."

"No harm done, Bear," I said with a fake smile, hoping to calm the situation.

"We're going to sit at the bar." City looked at Bear, not moving his eyes.

"Come on, dude, sit with us. Don't mind Bear. He's a total dick. Make his ass go sit at the bar," Frisco said.

"Sunshine and I want to be alone. I'll catch you guys another night," City said, pressing his hand against my back, guiding me away from the table and the large bar area.

"I'm sorry. They can be childish dicks. Bear doesn't have a filter," he said as he pulled out a chair for me. City had manners. Not many of the men I dated did something as simple as pull out a chair for a lady—it was a lost art. "He's a good guy, but sometimes his mouth runs and he doesn't think before he speaks."

"It's okay, really...it is. Thanks for sticking up for me," I said to him as I sat down, pulling my stool closer to the bar. "Why did you call me Sunshine?"

"Well, I don't know your name and you remind me of sunshine—your hair is golden and your smile glows. Just sounded right. I had to come up with something on the fly," he said. "I hope you didn't mind." He shrugged and grabbed the menu lying nearby.

"I didn't mind, but my name is Suzy."

"What would you like, Suzy?"

I wanted to say "you," because somehow this man made me lose my grip on reality. "Virgin daiquiri, please."

"Virgin? Really?" His brows shot up and the corner of his mouth twitched.

"I already had a drink tonight. I just want something sweet, no liquor."

"Do you want something to eat?" he asked. "You a vegetarian too?" He laughed.

"Shut up." I smacked him on the arm. "I'm good. I just want to call a tow truck."

"Gotcha." He pulled out his phone and placed it on the bar. "Hey, darlin', can you put in an order for a cheeseburger, a beer, and a virgin daiquiri?" he asked the bartender.

"Sure thing, handsome," she said, walking away, slowly swaying her hips to grab attention. I turned to City to see if he was watching her, but he was staring at me instead, and my mouth felt dry and scratchy.

"You want to call Triple A or someone else?" he asked without taking his eyes off me. They were an amazing shade of blue, and I couldn't look away. I'd always loved my blue eyes, but his were almost turquoise. I felt like he was staring through me, into me, seeing everything I hid under the surface. I wanted him, but I didn't want to admit my attraction. I couldn't admit it.

"Triple A is good," I said, reaching for my purse to find my membership card. I fumbled with my wallet, finding the card behind everything else inside. I could feel his eyes on me; he studied me and it made me nervous. What was he thinking? I dialed the number as I swiveled away from him, needing to avert his stare.

"Hello, Triple A, how can I help you?"

I could barely hear the tiny female voice above the loud classic rock that pulsed throughout the smoky bar. City chatted with the bartender as I tried to drown them out and give my location and details about my car. They wouldn't be able to make it out to my car until morning. Fuck. I thanked her for helping me before hitting the end button.

"What'd they say?" City asked with a sincere look as the bartender sashayed away from us.

"They won't make it out here until morning because they're busy and we're in the middle of nowhere. I'm to leave it unlocked so they can get in and put it in neutral or something. I don't know how it works. I've never had my car towed before." Now what the hell was I going to do? I was stranded at the Neon Cowboy with Mr. Sexalicious and my dirty thoughts.

"I'll bring you back to your car when I'm done eating. I guess you'll need a lift home too?" he asked, sipping his drink as he eyed me.

I smiled at him. Though I hated the thought of him going out of his way, and I wasn't that comfortable with a stranger knowing where I lived, I couldn't say no. "I'd appreciate it, if you don't mind."

"Not at all, Suzy. I can't just leave you here and walk out the door. I got ya, babe." He turned his stool toward me and leaned into my space. "Where do you want me to take you after we leave? Home?" He quirked an eyebrow, waiting for my response, and held me in place with his hard stare.

Home? Whose home was he referring to? City looked to be the type that had different women falling out of his bed every morning...or maybe he kicked them out before he fell asleep. His fingers brushed against the top of my hand and my internal dialogue evaporated.

"Where. Do. You. Live?" The laughter he tried to hide behind his hand made it clear that I'd sat there longer in thought than I had realized.

I cleared my throat. "I need to unlock my car then I need a lift home. I live about fifteen minutes north. Is that okay? I mean, I don't want to—" He put his finger over my lips and stopped me mid-sentence.

"Doesn't matter, I'll take you anywhere," he said with a sly grin that made my pulse race and my body heat. He licked his lips, and I stared like an idiot. My sex convulsed at the thought of his lips on my skin. What the fuck was wrong with me? Every movement he made and word he spoke turned sexual, as if permeating my brain. I needed to get laid; this man was not hitting on me, was he?

"You want some? I can't eat it all," he said as the plate was placed in front of him.

I shook my head and picked up my drink, trying to cool my body off from the internal fire caused by City. The cool, sweet strawberry slush danced across my tongue and slid down my throat.

I swirled the red straw in my mouth, trying to occupy my mind. His arms flexed as he lifted the burger to his mouth, forearms covered with tattoos. The left arm had various designs woven together—a koi fish, a tiger, and a couple of other nature-themed pieces that seemed to move across his skin, and his right arm had a city skyline. I wanted to touch his arms and run my fingers across his ink. He looked big everywhere, and my gaze drifted down his body and lingered at his crotch. I wondered if his motorcycle and tattoos made up for shortcomings elsewhere, but I couldn't believe a man like him was tiny. There was no way in hell he had a party...

"Pickle?"

I blinked and moved my eyes away from his crotch to his eyes. Pickle? He held it and motioned for me to take it.

"No. Thanks, though. You eat it," I said, feeling like he was reading my mind. God, I hoped he didn't see me staring at his crotch. I sucked down the rest of my drink, wishing now that it did have alcohol in it. Maybe then

I wouldn't feel so embarrassed. "I noticed your tattoos. What's the one on your right arm?"

"That's the Chicago skyline," he said, as he took another bite.

"You from there?"

"Born and bred, baby." He grunted and continued to chew. I couldn't take my eyes off his mouth. Watching him eat was erotic to me; his lips moved as he chewed, and he sucked each finger in his mouth to clean off the juices that flowed from the sandwich. Damn. It had been too long since I'd had sex—when eating becomes sexual.

Houston, we have a problem.

THROTTLE ME IS NOW AVAILABLE
Download the eBook for *FREE* at
chellebliss.com/inkedseries

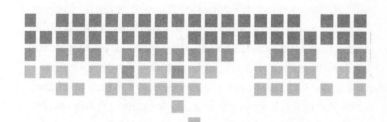

Acknowledgements

Sometimes I stare at this page for the longest amount of time and it never seems to get any easier either. There's a certain level or terror at the thought of forgetting someone. I don't want to be *that* asshole. When writing a book, it takes a small village working together before it becomes the book you're flipping through now. I have an entire team behind me, plus my readers, moving me forward to get shit done.

First and foremost, to my amazing readers and friends. Although I'd probably still write even if no one would read it, but I can't say thank you enough for actually spending your hard earned money to purchase Acquisition. I know you could've bought a Starbucks Frappucino and they're damn good. Especially the Venti Smores Fraps with coconut milk and the whip cream of course. I never forget that you made the decision to read my book instead of drinking two fraps which you'd eventually piss out anyway. I hope you had the same satisfaction as all that chocolatey goodness.

To my betas... God, there's so many of you. Thanks for the pep talk <insert sarcastic voice> after you read Acquisition. You're so patient waiting for book two. You ladies are my rock and help keep my ass straight when I'm ready to go off the rails.

Lisa, my editor and friend, you saved me so big. It didn't matter that I sent you the book with only two days to edit, you did it without complaining. You may have downed a gallon of wine in the process, but you did it because you love me. I can't thank you enough for putting up my insanity... Toni's too, but we all know which one of us is more sane or is it saner? Eh, that's my editors job ;).

To Julie, thank you for hopping on the proofreading of Acquisition and completing it in under 18 hour. You my friend are a rockstar. You pulled my ass out of a major jam. You're amazing at what you do and authors like myself with forever be thankful.

Fiona, what can I say? You're always there for me, toiling away with my mess. You've saved my ass a thousand times. You're not only an amazing proofreader, but a good friend. Thank you for everything, Fiona.

Kimberly Brower, my agent, thanks for putting up my insanity. The last year hasn't been easy, but thanks for being around when I need you. Thanks for helping put the Takeover Duet into motion and believing in me.

Meredith Wild, girl... Thank you for being you. You helped bring me back from a dark place. Writing Misadventures of a City Girl with you made me find my way again. The trip to Montreal and the watching our characters come to life did amazing things to my brain. I'm honored to call you a friend and I owe you more than you'll ever understand. Love ya hard, mama.

Sarah Hansen at Okay Creations, thank you for the beautiful cover. I wasn't easy to work with and was already a put short of a hole in one, but you rolled with it. I can't wait to get my hands on copies of the Takeover Duet because they're simply amazing.

To the people who hate me and wish to see me fail, go fuck yourself. No. Wait. Thank you. Why? Because you help propel me forward. I'm a gamblin' woman and you betting against my house only makes me dig harder and push deeper. So thanks for being an asshole.

To my reader Facebook group, Inked Addicts, thank you for always being amazeballs. I love each and every one of you and look forward to seeing what naughty things we can find.

To my friends like Aly Martinez, Mo Mabie, Meghan March, Mia Michelle, and others that I bother on a weekly basis... thank you for being the badest bitches around.

To my mom and family, I love you more than words can say. I would be nothing without your love and support. I'll be forever grateful to have you in my life.

To my dad and brother, I miss you more than anything in the world. I'd give up everything to have you back in my life. I hope, where ever you are, you're watching. I love you both.

To Brian, what can I say, boo? I loeve you.

To Tia Louise, chin up girl. Like can suck balls. I love you to the moon and back my sister in grief. Never forget you have an entire community behind you.

To all the people I forgot, I'm sorry. I guess I am *that* asshole. I promise I got your back the next time unless I forget.

Until next time... reach for the stars. Let no one tell you you're worth less than you are.

Love Always - Chelle, xoxo